Bolan caught the terrorist

The Executioner could have dropped the man easily, but alive he was more valuable to the warrior.

"Don't move," Bolan ordered from his prone position.

The gunner spun and triggered a burst in the direction of the voice. The slugs ripped through the branches above Bolan's head, showering him with leaves and splinters.

"I don't want to kill you!" the warrior shouted. "Toss the gun down."

The young man was so terrified that his breath came in gasps and sweat began to bead on his forehead. He jerked his head around, looking for the source of that terrible voice. Then with a gesture of surrender, he threw the Uzi to the ground.

As Bolan began to move out of cover, the gunner drew a pistol from an ankle holster, jammed the muzzle into his mouth and pulled the trigger.

Bolan looked on helplessly. The man had been afraid of his captor—but he had a greater fear of someone else....

MACK BOLAN®

The Executioner

DON PENDLETON'S
THE EXECUTIONER®
FEATURING MACK BOLAN®

DIRECT HIT

A GOLD EAGLE BOOK FROM
WORLDWIDE®

TORONTO • NEW YORK • LONDON • PARIS
AMSTERDAM • STOCKHOLM • HAMBURG
ATHENS • MILAN • TOKYO • SYDNEY

First edition September 1990

ISBN 0-373-61141-2

Special thanks and acknowledgment to
Carl Furst for his contribution to this work.

Printed in U.S.A.

Great men, great nations, have not been boasters
and buffoons, but perceivers of the terror of life, and
have manned themselves to face it.
—Ralph Waldo Emerson
The Conduct of Life, 1860

Men whose actions are motivated by greed often
perpetrate unspeakable acts. Terror mongers are
more often these days reaching out toward America.
Let them know here and now that I will face down
any terrorist threat to this great nation.
—Mack Bolan

To the families of U.S. servicemen
killed in Panama, December, 1989

Prologue

Mack Bolan felt relaxed, and accepted a light Scotch, from which he sipped sparingly. He'd come to Tel Aviv to meet Brognola after paying a visit to the Bekaa, and he felt somewhat satisfied about what had gone down. He toyed with the idea of a day or two R & R.

Feeling relaxed and the idea of a little R & R lasted about five minutes after he began to talk with the big Fed from Justice.

"Do you know what cesium 137 is?" Brognola asked.

"I've got some idea. What's it all about?"

The burly man from the Department of Justice chewed intently on the beleaguered cigar he held between his teeth. "It's damned dangerous stuff. It's used for cancer therapy. The machine the doctor, or technician, uses is a big lead-lined cylinder that can be moved over the table where the patient lies. There's a hole about the size of a quarter in the bottom of that cylinder, and it's got a lead cap over it. When they move the cap aside, the radiation streams out and into the patient's body. They give the patient that stream of radiation for just a little time, and usually it does kill at least part of the cancer."

"I remember a report about cesium being stolen somewhere in Brazil a while back."

"You got it, Striker. A small amount of cesium 137 was stolen by junk dealers who had no idea what it was. They only wanted the container for its value as junk. When they broke it open and broke open the stainless steel capsule inside, they found the stuff, in the form of a handful of powder. Cesium 137 glows with a pretty red-blue light. The townspeople didn't have a clue about what it was, and smeared it on their bodies and danced in the streets.

"It killed them. The radioactivity was so intense that the bodies of the victims had to be buried in heavy lead-lined caskets. Houses had to be bulldozed to the ground, then the rubble hauled away and buried deep. Household pets and other domestic animals had to be killed and buried. Whole areas of the town were abandoned."

"Hal, are you telling me that someone stole a quantity of cesium 137?"

"Yeah. From a cancer clinic in New York."

"Any idea what for?" Bolan asked.

"Cesium 137 has nothing to do with making bombs," Brognola replied, "which is a bit of a relief. It's a by-product of a nuclear reactor, and let me tell you, it's one of the most highly radioactive substances in the world. It's an isotope, man-made—doesn't occur in nature. What they might want to do with it? The prospects are terrifying."

"Any idea who has it?"

"No, but we've got some suggestive intel. The clinic had a night watchman, a young guy who worked for a security company. He was shot, but he'll survive. He got a glimpse of the man who shot him. An Oriental, he said, and guessed him for Japanese. Dark business suit. Close-cropped hair. The guy shot him without a word, and probably thought he killed him."

"So what did we learn from that?" Bolan asked.

"The slug the doctor dug out of the young man's chest is a 7.62 mm, and it was fired from a CZ-52. Your garden-variety American burglars don't carry Czech pistols."

"And your garden-variety world terrorists do," Bolan suggested.

"You got it."

1

Mack Bolan turned in his seat and glanced uneasily out the rear window of the car. The convoy was spread out over too much highway. The armored truck following two hundred yards back was carrying fissionable plutonium, the "stuff" atomic bombs were made of, and if the French expected trouble, they were guarding that dangerous material in a casual, even amateurish way.

The first car of the convoy was running so far ahead that it was out of sight most of the time, supposedly clearing the way. It ran with its blue emergency light blinking, and a loudspeaker mounted on its roof. An officer with a microphone was warning all southbound traffic to pull to the side of the road until the northbound convoy passed by.

The second car, filled with armed policemen, was about a hundred yards ahead. Robert Rousseau, the senior French policeman Bolan wanted to talk to, was riding in that car.

The warrior sat in the back seat of the third car, beside Paul Lemaire, an agent of Groupe d'Intervention de la Gendarmerie Nationale, the special French counterterrorist force. Two uniformed police officers occupied the front, both armed with MAT 49s, French submachine guns, as well as the Berettas.

A squat blue police van followed a hundred yards or so behind, carrying heavy weapons and radio equipment.

Still another hundred yards back, the heavy-armored truck rolled ponderously along the highway. Five helmeted soldiers with heavy weapons perched on top.

One final police car brought up the rear.

The convoy was spread out over a mile of highway—the six vehicles of the main body were spread out over almost half a mile. There was little traffic on this scenic mountain highway. Anyone wishing to get anywhere in a hurry chose a faster, more direct route.

The convoy could have taken another highway, but this one was better for the purpose. Traffic would be less likely to be disrupted, and there was less chance of causing panic or encountering protesters. And if there was an accident, there would be less chance of injury or death. Except to the personnel of the convoy.

Fortunately, the move was being made in secret. If the time and route had been made public, the protesters would have organized, tried to stop the run, waved their signs, yelling, chanting…defying the gendarmerie to move them.

Bolan knew the orders that the drivers had—move through, even if you have to drive over a mob of peaceniks or nukeniks. And he knew these drivers would do it. They were specially picked; they were tough.

"We appreciate your coming to France," Lemaire said.

Bolan only glanced at him and didn't reply. He hadn't come to do a favor for the French, especially not for Paul Lemaire. He'd come because Hal Brognola had asked him to. What was going on throughout the world right now looked bad. It gave terrorism a new face, and for right now, it looked as if the key to it might be found in France.

The warrior had flown from Tel Aviv to Athens and from there to Nice. He'd come to meet with Robert Rousseau, who knew more about the new threat than anyone else in France. He had arrived just in time, it turned out, to find

Rousseau about to leave with his convoy. If someone decided to attack it, Rousseau had explained, he wanted to see how it was done.

They had driven north into the mountains to the site of the French nuclear reactor that produced the fissionable plutonium. Rousseau hadn't yet explained why the plutonium was being moved, when they encountered Lemaire, who was also part of the convoy. Lemaire had insisted *he* wanted to talk with Bolan.

So here he was, riding in a car with Lemaire instead of with Rousseau. He knew Lemaire, had run up against him before—and that had been no great pleasure.

"The pattern is growing clearer," Lemaire said. "The terrorists are stealing the most dangerous kinds of radioactive materials. We—"

"Gare!" the driver shrieked.

Bolan didn't need the warning. He'd seen the flash of the launcher and the bright flame of the rocket streaking toward the car just ahead. The missile smashed into the vehicle's right front door and exploded, glass and sheet metal spewing out of fire and smoke.

Lemaire's driver slammed on the brakes, and the car skidded.

Bolan jerked open his door and dived to the ground before the sedan came to a stop, followed closely by Lemaire.

The car had spun around as it skidded, and the second missile hit it just above the front bumper. The explosion tossed the car three feet into the air, and when it touched down it was a shattered heap of torn steel.

Bolan raced for the shoulder of the highway and threw himself into the ditch. A second later he was on his knees, peering over the lip toward where he'd seen the flash of the launcher.

He could make out two hardmen, working over their tube, preparing to let loose another rocket.

He took aim with his .44 Magnum, but before he could get off a shot he was hit by the shock of a powerful explosion, much bigger than the two eruptions that had demolished the cars.

The terrorists had blown the bridge the convoy was crossing.

It was a clever maneuver—the armored truck hadn't crossed, but most of the police vehicles had. Now the bridge was down, and the truck and its hazardous cargo was cut off from what remained of the police force that was supposed to guard it.

Heavy machine guns suddenly opened fire. The soldiers on top of the truck returned fire, but they were exposed and outgunned.

A third rocket slammed into the van. The policemen had expected the attack, and had scrambled out of the vehicle.

Bolan aimed at the point where he'd seen the last flash. It was a long shot, but the Executioner was a marksman.

The Desert Eagle thundered an authoritative roar, its muzzle-flash visible even in the bright sunlight.

One of the terrorists screamed in horror when he saw his confederate's head and shoulders explode into bloody fragments.

Lemaire was in the ditch on the other side of the highway, sweeping the roadside with bursts from a mini-Uzi. One of the policemen from the front seat was on his knees beside him, firing a MAT 49.

The policemen in the van were firing back across the bridge, trying to cut down the terrorists who had taken command of the armored truck and its load of plutonium. The last police car of the convoy had been crippled by machine-gun fire. One man was crouched on the far side, returning fire, but it looked as if the other officers were dead.

The surviving terrorist had abandoned the launcher and the body of his accomplice. He had slid down a slope into the cover of roadside weeds and brush, and Lemaire and the policeman strafed the area with bursts of 9 mm slugs.

Bolan climbed out of the ditch and raced toward the wreckage of the car ahead. In a moment he knew that he'd never finish his conversation with Robert Rousseau. The Frenchman was sprawled half out of the car, with his head and shoulders down on the road. That was all that remained recognizable. The officer who had been sitting in the rear seat with him had been decapitated by flying steel.

Only the woman driver was alive. She lay on the pavement outside the vehicle, moaning weakly. Both her legs were gone, and the ground around her glistened with her blood. She was dying.

Bolan knelt beside her, and her lips moved.

Her eyes focused for a moment on the big man. *"Papa..."* she whispered.

BOLAN STOOD UP and took quick stock of the situation. Orders were being shouted, punctuated by the yells and screams of the wounded. Automatic weapons still chattered. The lead car of the convoy had come rushing back, and four policemen jumped out, brandishing their weapons and looking for targets.

And on the other side of the bridge, the armored truck, carrying high-grade plutonium, disappeared around a curve in the highway.

Bolan sprinted across the pavement to the place where the terrorist crew had fired the rockets. The man he'd shot with the .44 Magnum lay sprawled on the ground, dead. He had been lying prone when the bullet plowed into him, and it created a ghastly wound.

The warrior looked around the battle zone. Lemaire and the other French policemen had discovered more gunmen on the other side of the road and were in pursuit, laying down heavy fire as they ran up and into the woods.

Bolan trotted down to the little stream where the rocket gunner had retreated. It wasn't difficult to see where the man had left the stream and struggled up the far slope, about twenty yards south. He was struggling—afraid, hurried, obsessed with escape—and so he was careless.

The Executioner was also a hunter. He'd been hunted often enough and knew what went through both minds. This man was tormented by the vision of his accomplice literally exploding beside him, knew the man had been taken out by no clumsy gendarme spraying the area with automatic fire. Whoever had killed his confederate had fired a single shot at long range, and the hunted man was afraid.

For his kind, killing was easy. The thought of *being* killed tore up his guts, made him panic.

The guy had clawed his way up from the little stream and run headlong into the wood, leaving a clear trail.

What he would do was clear enough, too. He'd run until he was exhausted, or until he thought his pursuer was catching up; then he'd set himself for a clear shot at the man coming after him, try to drop him before the pursuer knew what was happening.

Bolan made his way quietly through the woods, stopping now and then to listen. Let the hunted man run. He'd tire.

After a while Bolan could hear him thrashing through the trees and knew the man was losing ground. Sooner or later, the fugitive would try to circle back to where he'd stashed his vehicle. It had to be on a side road a little way back to avoid detection.

The pulsing horns of police vehicles began to sound in the distance.

Bolan knew the hunted man's vehicle had to be to the south. He couldn't escape to the north—the bridge was out, and he and his accomplice had known it would be. So, he'd circle to the south.

The warrior's quarry thrashed his way toward the road. He'd pass Bolan only a little to the left. The time had come to move.

To create a diversion, Bolan picked up a branch and tossed it about twenty yards ahead of the gunner. It fell with a clatter, and the man let fly a burst of slugs. Bolan knelt on one knee and peered into the woods, catching a glimpse of the man through the brush. He could have dropped him easily enough, but the warrior wanted him alive.

The man fired another burst.

Bolan lay down on the ground. "Don't move," he ordered.

The terrorist spun and fired a burst toward the voice. The slugs ripped through the branches above Bolan, showering him with leaves and splinters.

"Speak English?"

The gunner remained silent.

Bolan could see him clearly now. His quarry was a young man with a Mediterranean complexion.

"I don't want to kill you," Bolan told him. "I think you know enough English to understand that."

Silence.

"Toss the gun down."

The young man stared toward his adversary. His weapon was an Uzi, and he swung the muzzle back and forth, looking for a target.

"Drop it," Bolan ordered. "Remember what happened to your partner."

The young man breathed hard. He was so terrified that his breath came in gasps and the sweat began to bead his forehead. He jerked his head around, looking for the origin of the voice. Then, with a gesture of surrender, he threw the Uzi to the ground.

"Good. That's smart. Now take off your clothes." Bolan had seen all kinds of deadly little weapons whipped out of pockets or small holsters hidden on the body. He didn't intend to become a victim of an oversight.

The young man bent over as if he were unfastening his pants, suddenly he jerked a pistol from an ankle holster.

Before Bolan could move, the terrorist jammed the muzzle of the pistol into his mouth and pulled the trigger.

He had been afraid of his captor—but he'd had a greater fear of something else.

BROGNOLA ARRIVED in Nice the next morning. He met with Paul Lemaire and other representatives of GIGN and Police Judiciare, and later joined Bolan at a sidewalk café.

"They got away with enough high-grade plutonium to make three or four bombs," the big Fed announced as soon as he sat down at the wrought iron table.

"And these days even a high school physics student can make a bomb, given the facilities and materials. And this crowd, whoever they are, now has the material," Bolan concluded.

The warrior frowned over the classified report Brognola had given him to read. Although the attack on the convoy in the South of France couldn't be kept quiet, the public hadn't yet been told what had been stolen. The government feared panic.

He finished scanning the typewritten pages, then shook his head. "French security was amateurish. They'd move gold with better security techniques than that. The convoy was spread out a mile.''

"Well, there was nothing amateurish about the coordinated attack.''

"Yeah,'' Bolan said thoughtfully. His frown deepened. "You know, though, the French security would have been enough, except for one thing.''

"Which is?''

Bolan slapped the report down on the coffee table in front of Brognola. "The terrorists knew when the plutonium was being moved, over what routes, and how the convoy would be spread out. There's no coincidence in this. They knew!''

"The same idea has occurred to the French,'' Brognola replied.

"And because of their leaky security, every major city is in danger.''

"They've put their very best people on it,'' Brognola told him. "Police Judiciare. Plus—'' he paused to emphasize the significance of what he was about to add "—GIGN. You know GIGN.''

"Only too well.''

"They hunt down the enemies of France and simply kill them,'' Brognola added.

"I suppose they respect terrorists' rights at least as much as those terrorists respected the rights of the French police they killed on that highway.''

Bolan reached for a cup of coffee. "Where does it go from here?'' he asked.

"I'd appreciate it if you'd stay in France and work with Lemaire for a little while. For the moment, GIGN has better leads than we have.''

The warrior nodded.

"There've been other thefts of radioactive material. You know we'd had two in the States within the past month.

Well, we've had two more. Radioactive sludge from nuclear plants, stuff on its way to being buried. It's no good for bomb making. Just deadly dangerous radioactive sludge.

"You can play a lot of dirty tricks with stuff like that," Brognola continued. "We can see a pattern in it now. It's not just chance. Somebody is developing a scheme."

"Since?"

"Since maybe a month ago. Six weeks. Let me show you something."

Brognola reached into his briefcase and pulled out a bulging file. He laid out a group of photographs on the coffee table.

"Iraq," he said. "Look at this."

He pushed the first 8 x 10 toward Bolan and pointed at what appeared to be the opening of some caves in a dry valley. Trucks and tents stood before the cave entrances.

"The word to the shepherds and goatherds who have used this valley for centuries is don't go near the caves. Something evil is lurking there. The shepherds figured it was the same evil that was always there—the loot that generations of robbers have hidden. So some of them went in to see what they could find. They later died of radiation sickness, which of course they had no idea they had. Doctors from Baghdad were the ones who identified it.

"Look at this picture," Brognola went on, shoving another print toward Bolan. "A burned-out truck. Look at the bullet holes. Somebody doesn't want anyone near the caves."

"Looks that way," Bolan agreed.

"Okay, let's keep looking. Look at what's being loaded into this DC-3."

Drums were being lifted by heavy forklift trucks. Equipment that heavy wasn't needed to lift barrels of oil.

"Lead-lined drums, you figure?"

Brognola shrugged. "Ain't oil, buddy. Or gasoline. Or insecticide. And where the hell do you suppose they're flying whatever is in those drums?"

"Next picture," Bolan suggested.

Brognola shook his head. "We don't know where they flew off to. Our informant says the drums came from the caves. That's all we know."

"I knew it wouldn't be easy," the warrior said dryly.

"One more picture. Here's the man who tipped us off, along with his government. Not out of patriotism, you understand. The storage of radioactive materials in the caves interferes with the way of life he follows, his father followed, his grandfather followed, and for all he knows the same back to Adam. You just might meet him again sometime. You ought to remember his face."

Bolan stared at the solemn, weathered face of an Iraqi herder. He stood proud in this picture, most likely the first photograph ever taken of him. He was proud of his weapon, a Kalashnikov assault rifle that could fire single shots or bursts as the man wanted.

"His name is Ali Ibrahim," Brognola said. "The way he sees it, the city boys from Baghdad are somehow dumping their poison on country boys like him, and he doesn't like it. He doesn't give a damn for the government in Baghdad, or their wars. All he's interested in is being able to shelter in those caves with his herd on cold winter nights."

"Which makes him a valuable informer," Bolan observed.

"I wish we had as good ones in other places. Radioactive material has been stolen in South Africa, India and Canada. Until now, nobody thought of the stuff as anything anybody'd want to steal. Now it's a pattern. It's a new dimension of terrorism, Striker. I figured you'd be interested."

Bolan blew a loud breath. "France."

"For the time being. But be ready for the call. I might have to call you home or someplace else, any minute. You willing?"

"Sure, Hal. Same as always."

2

Self-styled general and President-for-life Taiyodi Laqiya stood in the middle of the showplace VIP lounge of his new airport in the desert south of Sidi, which was the name of both his capital and his nation. Built to resemble a Bedouin tent, the structure nevertheless featured an immense expanse of glass on the side facing the main runway, which made it possible for General Laqiya to watch the arrival of aircraft and to see the passengers disembark and walk across the hot tarmac to the air-conditioned haven of the terminal.

He wore a long white robe, embroidered with green and gold threads in elaborate loops and swirls at the neck and wrists. On his head he wore a white *keffiyeh*, held in place by an *akal*, the traditional Arab headdress, and his eyes were hidden behind large sunglasses.

"That is Isoroku Akada," murmured the man at the general's side, his aide Nasira Fouzi. "He's called the Shark."

The short, heavyset, dark-skinned Laqiya nodded as if he'd already known that the Japanese who stepped down from the small jet was the Shark.

The arrival of the Shark all but completed the list of guests. Albrecht Kirchner was sitting in the lounge, relaxing over a glass of brandy. He would accompany Akada in the limousine for the drive to the conference center.

Abu Vilad, who had arrived two hours ago, had gone on to the center, a sumptuous hotel disguised as a mud-hut village in a narrow, rocky valley. He had brought his women and his wine, and obviously he meant to enjoy both while waiting for his fellow conferees. The Italian, Balbo Manero, was there too.

The only man not accounted for was Hajan Dihanesi, the Iranian. There was no news of him.

General Laqiya walked toward the door through which the Japanese would enter the lounge. He could see him through the glass door: a compact, wiry man, typically Japanese. He wore a black Western business suit, carried a black briefcase and was followed by an obsequious second Japanese, who carried a large case.

The general was prepared with a speech of welcome. It was in Japanese and phonetically written out for him. As the Shark walked into the lounge, Laqiya grabbed and shook his hand, then stepped back and began his speech.

Kirchner walked past Laqiya and shook hands with Isoroku Akada. He spoke to him in English, which the general couldn't understand. The Japanese nodded enthusiastically as the German spoke. Then abruptly the two of them strode past the startled Laqiya and walked toward the exit door.

"Rudeness!" the general's aide muttered.

"Quiet, Nasira," Laqiya replied. "Do you want to tell them they're rude? They're killers, and two of the most dangerous men you have ever seen."

"And they and the others will betray us, Great Leader," Nasira said under his breath. "They'll use us and never deliver the fissionable material."

Taiyodi Laqiya watched the two men leave the lounge and walk toward the waiting limousine. "Never mind," he said to his aide. "Their coming here will prove of great benefit to us. One way or another."

Fouzi watched with narrowed eyes. He doubted that a visit by such men as these would prove of any benefit, either to the Great Leader or to Sidi. It might, though, prove to be of substantial benefit to Nasira Fouzi. The Shark and the Knife. Akada and Kirchner. Yes, someone would pay well for the information that these two men were in Sidi. And if they liked that information well enough, he could perhaps sell some more names. Fouzi smiled. He could even sell names of men who didn't appear for this meeting.

INTERPOL HEADQUARTERS is a bland modern office building in the Paris suburb of Saint Cloud. There, on the same day when the chief men of the United Righteous were meeting in a clandestine but luxurious conference center in Sidi, representatives of the world's leading antiterrorist organizations met to design a plan for fighting a new terrorist threat.

The meeting was dead secret. Every man and woman attending the conference was the subject of a cover story if necessary, ranging from a news release to the effect that Monsieur So-and-So had entered a hospital for the removal of a benign polyp from his intestines to a tabloid splash purporting to show Colonel Somebody-Else disporting himself with an anonymous half-nude female on a tropical beach.

Hal Brognola represented the United States at the conference.

France was represented by Paul Lemaire of GIGN. The British representative was Major Harold Johnson, a somewhat shadowy figure who was identified both with MI-6 and SAS. SAS, Special Air Service, was reputedly as close to a GIGN as the British government could have. The Federal

Republic of Germany—West Germany—was represented by Heinrich Schumann, an officer of an organization with the horrendous name of Bundesnachtrichtendienst, BND, which was the German military Intelligence service. Italy was represented by Galeazzo Pitocco of SISDE, the Italian antiterrorist Intelligence service.

The Japanese government was represented, as were the Australians, the Spanish, the Swiss and the Egyptians.

Present, too, though only as an official observer, was Natalya Mikhailovna Kornilov, vaguely identified as an agent of the KGB.

The meeting began over lunch, with too many toasts. Hal Brognola had little confidence in meetings, particularly meetings of this size, and he looked forward to a much smaller session later, with a much smaller cast of characters that could include Mack Bolan.

He had some ominous news for him. In a second attack, at a hospital in Cleveland, more cesium 137 had been stolen.

ABU VILAD HANDED a note to Albrecht Kirchner:

Our meeting room is undoubtedly bugged. Pass this note around, please.

Kirchner nodded and passed the note on to the other conferees.

"They are alert," Abu Vilad began. "They are meeting in Paris today to talk about what to do. It would be a mistake for us to assume they are incapable of acting. If, for example, they knew we were here today, I think it entirely possible we would be bombed by American carrier planes from their Atlantic fleet."

"In which case," Kirchner said, "everything would be triggered. We would be avenged."

"A comforting thought," Vilad added dryly.

Abu Vilad was a Palestinian, second-in-command of an organization known as ISF, Islamic Strike Force. There were fewer than a hundred men in the ISF, but they had succeeded in two years in making themselves the most feared and hated terrorist organization in the world. They had shot down a fully loaded El Al 747, with hand-launched heat-seeking missiles; they had detonated a bomb in the transfer lounge at Leonardo da Vinci Airport, killing thirty-four young American Jews on their way to a kibbutz in Israel; they had attempted to assassinate the Israeli delegate to a UNESCO conference in Geneva. That they had failed in an attempt to throw a bomb onto the trading floor of the New York Stock Exchange hadn't made them less feared or hated. Identified members of the ISF were hunted down and killed without arrest or trial. It had lost more than a quarter of its original members in two years, but volunteers had come forward to replace them.

Abu Vilad was forty years old, which was old for a member of the ISF. In appearance he was an unprepossessing man: short, slight, bald, with a small black mustache that didn't make him look fierce or bold. He wore gold-rimmed round eyeglasses. Today he was dressed in a simple khaki shirt and khaki pants. Unprepossessing though he might be, it would have been a mistake for anyone to underestimate him. Only four months ago he had settled a leadership question in the ISF by drawing a pistol in a meeting and shooting a dissident to death on the spot.

"We have succeeded," Manero said. "We have all the radioactive materials we need. And, incidentally, our compliments, Akada, on an exceptionally clean operation in seizing the cesium 137 out of that New York cancer clinic. That was exceptionally well done.''

"I thank you, *signor*,"

"But a question remains unresolved," Manero added.

"Many questions remain unresolved," Akada replied.

Manero nodded at Akada. "Yes. The big agenda or the little agenda. I had in mind a more immediate question. Do we speak first or act first?"

"I think there is no question about that," Abu Vilad said. "We effect a demonstration first. *Then* we tell them what price they will have to pay to avoid a second demonstration."

"I agree," Akada said.

"Then where is this demonstration? And what?" Kirchner asked.

Vilad smiled. "Tel Aviv."

Akada bowed toward Vilad and duplicated his wry smile. "Patience, my friend. The most effective demonstration would not be against Israel. The world is accustomed to thinking of Israel as a target. One more demonstration of the people's anger against the Zionists..." He shrugged. "The world is capable of shaking it off. But if we choose a target that—"

"That excludes the United States, too, then," Vilad interrupted.

Akada nodded. "For the moment. No. I suggest we make our demonstration against someone not known as an enemy. It will seem irrational. Inexplicable. Let the world see that no one is safe, that no one can look on with a detached air while the righteous wrath of the oppressed is directed exclusively against nations like the United States and Israel."

"Where, then?" Manero queried.

Isoroku Akada lifted a slight shrug and showed a cryptic little smile. "Let us use my cesium for our demonstration," he said. "Everything man fears can come from a tiny quantity of that material."

FIVE MEN MET in a conference room in police headquarters in Paris. Besides Bolan, Brognola and a British major, Harold Johnson, another man was present, a man who hadn't attended the meeting at Interpol headquarters in Paris. He was David Syrkin, officially representing no one but understood to be an agent of Mossad—Israeli Intelligence.

Brognola was impatient with meetings. Bolan was more so. In his judgment, little was accomplished in most of them, and he was anxious to be on the move. He'd come here to get intel, and he hoped they didn't take too long producing it.

Lemaire was a chain-smoker and a heavy drinker, and his self-indulgence made him look older than he really was. He was in his thirties, but his puffy face and drooping eyelids gave him the look of a man in his fifties.

"Police Judiciare," he said, "are arriving at a suspicion about the identity of the men who attacked the convoy and stole the plutonium. Have you heard of an organization called Islamic Strike Force?"

"We have heard of it," Brognola replied grimly.

"The field commander," Lemaire continued, "is one Abu Vilad, a shadowy figure who hides from the light. The commander-in-chief is even more hidden. But we have learned who he is."

"Recently?" Major Johnson asked.

"Actually," Lemaire said, "it is David's friends who have learned the identity."

David Syrkin was a tall, husky, curly haired young man with a careless air that suggested he took almost nothing seriously. He smiled when his name was mentioned, put his wineglass aside, and said, "A man caught trying to plant a bomb in a school for young children, about three weeks ago, elected to tell us who's the head man of ISF. We know who he is and where he is."

"A Lebanese businessman," Lemaire said.

"Supposed to be. In fact, he's a lifelong terrorist, a man without a country, with no loyalty to anyone, who practices terrorism for profit and lives very well off it."

"What is his name?"

Syrkin shrugged. "Who knows? He calls himself Napoleon Malik. He pretends to be a broker in Lebanese wines, olives and the like. He lives in Montparnasse, here in Paris."

"And what does he have to do with the attack on the convoy and the theft of the plutonium?" Bolan asked.

"The missile that blew up the car leading the plutonium convoy is a Czech weapon called a Pancerovka," Lemaire said. "Fragments have identified the rocket bomb. This weapon has become obsolete, and so it's sold to Asian and African countries. We were able to trace this particular model of the Pancerovka to the year 1971 and even to the month of manufacture. Ones like it have been captured in the fighting along the border between Mali and Sidi, in the hands of Sidian troops. We also know that the president of Sidi supplies weapons to the ISF."

"Something to go on," Bolan agreed, "but—"

"But not enough," Syrkin interrupted. "We can do better. Rounds fired in the assault on the convoy have been ballistically matched to rounds fired in the ISF attack on the Israeli delegate's car in Geneva. Two of the criminals were killed in that attack, and at least two got away. The Uzi used by one of them was used again in the assault on the convoy."

"Very interesting police work," Major Johnson commended.

"It's how we survive," Syrkin said.

"Maybe the time has come to do something about Mr. Napoleon Malik," Brognola suggested.

"We have already decided this," Lemaire told him. "We want to take him alive. Then we might find out where the plutonium has gone."

"I've volunteered to help," Syrkin said.

"Perhaps," said Major Johnson, "it would be well if Mr. Bolan takes part in the operation. I suppose the point is to have the best team available. Will you assign him to it, Mr. Brognola?"

Brognola grinned. "I don't give him assignments. Mack works independently. And unofficially."

"I assume GIGN has its own specialists," the warrior said.

"It's a difficult and risky operation," Lemaire replied. "Taking him alive, I mean. I've seen you work, Monsieur Bolan. I'd like to have you with me."

Bolan glanced around the table. He nodded. "Okay. Deal me in."

"DON'T COUNT ON THIS to be easy," Bolan said to Lemaire after he had his first look at the apartment building where Napoleon Malik lived in the Fourteenth Arrondissement, Montparnasse, directly south of the Seine, southwest of the cathedral of Notre Dame de Paris.

The building was on a brick-paved street lined with a few chestnut trees, in a neighborhood only a few blocks from the famous Montparnasse Cemetery. Napoleon Malik had chosen his residence well. Upper-level management types lived in the area—men who didn't want to commute long distances from the Second Arrondissement, the central district of French finance and business. GIGN knew who else lived in the building—a banker, a prosperous lawyer, a broker in iron and steel. The presence of a Lebanese broker in such products as wines and olives was nothing unusual to his neighbors.

Neither was his family. His neighbors couldn't have guessed that Malik's "wife" was a drug dealer he had bought from the warden of a filthy Pakistani prison after she had been publicly flogged in the dust of the forecourt of a mosque. She was a striking young woman, with a rigid, erect posture and studied dignity. To all appearances they were a conservative Middle Eastern family, struggling to live comfortably as refugees from a world that had fallen apart.

This was known to the French authorities. What hadn't been known until Mossad told them was that Napoleon Malik was the mysterious chief of ISF.

That explained something Police Judiciare had learned during its recent intensive investigation—that three apartments out of the eight in the building, Malik's apartment and two others, were leased by a company called Produits du Levant, "Products of the Middle East." The other two apartments were occupied by officers of the company.

Bolan figured that the "officers" were more likely hardmen.

"That," said Lemaire, "leaves five apartments occupied by innocent French civilians. You see my problem, Monsieur Bolan? It's why I have asked for you and Syrkin to help. Ah, we of GIGN can blast our way in. But—"

"You get him outside," Bolan finished, "before he goes in. Or after he comes out."

"We watch. He comes and goes at odd hours, always with men around him, and some of them are dressed like him, to confuse assassins."

"It's not just the law that wants him," Bolan said. "There's always somebody who wants the blood of a guy like that."

"It will have to be a surgical operation," Syrkin warned.

"Easy to say. So how do we go about it?" Lemaire asked.

"When he comes and goes, is it always in the same car?" Syrkin probed.

Lemaire shook his head. "They use three cars."

"You follow them all?" Bolan asked.

"Yes. Sometimes we lose one, but we follow all three. Sometimes they stop and men change from one car to another."

"All right," Bolan said. "Here's what I suggest . . ."

NAPOLEON MALIK WAS only the most recent name the man had used. Since he was fourteen years old he had changed his name at least once every year—so often that he hardly remembered the name his parents had given him, no more than he remembered the parents he'd last seen when he was six years old. He had used this name Malik longer than he'd used any other, for almost four years now. It suited him. He liked it.

The woman called herself Jasmin Malik. As good a name as any. He never carried a weapon. She carried two, so she could pass one to him if an emergency arose where he would need it. She accompanied him everywhere he went. Though she was ostensibly his wife, he had no marital relations with her. The truth was, she was his bodyguard.

Malik was an Arab, and as such had a dark complexion and dark eyes. He was a big man, tall and a little too heavy, and his double-breasted suits made him look bulkier than he actually was.

On Tuesday evening they sat in a Lebanese restaurant on the north slope of Montmartre. Malik read an Arabic newspaper. Jasmin, playing subdued and dutiful wife, sat across the table, waiting. She wore trousers and a jacket of green silk, and her head was covered with a white silk scarf embroidered with gold thread.

"Ah," she said. "He is here."

Malik looked up, recognized Abu Vilad and put his paper aside. Vilad approached the table, nodded a greeting to both of them and sat down.

"It went well," he reported.

"What demands?"

"Actually, none. Next week, a demonstration."

"The general paid?"

"A million francs. In return I gave him no promise. But he's literally slavering over the prospect of getting his hands on fissionable plutonium."

Malik smiled. "He would use it. If he had a bomb, he would use it."

"Isoroku Akada proposes we kill him."

"Sooner or later."

"Later," Vilad said. "First we get more money."

"Yes. The money?"

"In the usual three accounts in Zurich. The usual three-way split."

"Another reason the general must die sooner or later," Malik told him. "If he turns against us, he'll tell how much he paid. Our associates must never find out that General Laqiya gave us a million, not just the half million you put in the ISF account."

"Their minds don't go to that sort of thing." Vilad picked up a menu from the table. "Let's eat. We have much business to talk about later. But not of course here."

"THERE'S THE FIRST CAR," Lemaire pointed. "That's the one he left in this morning."

"Is that him?" Syrkin asked, nodding toward the husky, swarthy man in a double-breasted suit who got out of the rear seat in the light blue Mercedes and walked into the apartment building.

"I don't think so," Lemaire replied. "But we'll soon know."

Bolan, Lemaire and Syrkin were inside a telephone service van parked half a block from the building. They were dressed in the blue coveralls worn by nearly all French laborers, which gave them good cover for their weapons. Bolan had his .44 Magnum Desert Eagle automatic holstered under the loose coveralls. Syrkin had a mini-Uzi.

Earlier in the day some real workmen had opened two manholes in the pavement of the street and had placed yellow barriers around them. Now, in the darkness of midevening, little yellow lights flashed on the barriers. To give added reality to the idea that the underground telephone cables were being repaired, workmen had interrupted telephone service to the apartment building from time to time. It was interrupted now.

Permission had been secured from the owner of the apartment adjoining Malik's for the installation of spike microphones in the wall. With the microphones in place, conversations could be clearly heard in the earphones worn by a GIGN agent also sitting in the van.

"Malik?" Lemaire asked the man with the earphones.

The man shook his head and said in French that the man who had just entered the building hadn't gone to Malik's apartment.

"A clever man, Monsieur Malik," Lemaire said. "He varies his routine, uses different cars, comes and goes at odd hours. But he isn't so clever. When it really is him he's accompanied by the woman."

The radio in the front seat crackled. The driver picked up the headset, listened and talked.

"Is okay," he said in English. "Is from the restaurant the black Mercedes leaving. Is five people. Is four when came. A man joins these people."

"Is one of them the woman?" Lemaire asked.

The man asked in French and listened to the answer. Then he said, "Yes. Is the woman. Tall, dark, pretty."

"Time to go underground, gentlemen," Bolan said.

"Not yet," Lemaire replied. "It will take half an hour for the car to come here from Montmartre."

They waited, receiving by radio a running report from the team that tailed the black Mercedes. When the car crossed the river and entered boulevard Saint Michel, Lemaire said it was time to move.

Bolan, Lemaire and Syrkin walked quickly to the manhole nearest the van and descended into the brick-walled utility tunnel beneath the street. It was dark down there, and they used flashlights to move forward. The pavement under their feet was wet. The walls and ceiling were lined with pipes and cables.

Lemaire carried a Handie-Talkie and continued to hear the report from the GIGN cars that were tailing the Mercedes. When the vehicle turned onto this street, the way would be blocked at both ends by police cars that were standing by. Other policemen were inside the apartment building and would block the entry. Malik and his group would be trapped. Bolan, Lemaire and Syrkin would then emerge from the manhole nearest the building and confront them.

This was the plan. It left Malik no way to escape—assuming that the man in the black Mercedes *was* Malik. He'd be challenged on the street with superior force, and unless he was totally insane he'd surrender.

Bolan had edged his way to the front as the group reached the ladder under the manhole, which made him the man at the top of the ladder, keeping his head just below the level of the pavement.

They waited. Lemaire had turned the sound level to its lowest setting, so the squawk of the Handie-Talkie wouldn't be heard on the street. But he could hear the transmissions, and he tensed suddenly.

"Now."

Bolan rose up and peered above ground. His face was caught in the glare of the headlights on the black Mercedes, and for an instant he wondered if the big car was about to run over the manhole. Then it swerved toward the curb.

The warrior scrambled out, followed by Lemaire and Syrkin. Crouched around the manhole, weapons drawn and ready, they were on the driver's side of the car.

The doors opened on the passenger side of the sedan, and someone got out on the sidewalk in front of the red brick apartment building.

Suddenly a blast of gunfire erupted from the Mercedes. Someone in the vehicle had spotted the police cars moving into position. The officers in the door went down, and all hell broke loose.

A grenade was tossed out of the window behind the driver's seat and rolled across the pavement.

Bolan threw himself to the street, knocking down Lemaire. Syrkin got off a burst from his mini-Uzi before he, too, dived to the pavement.

The lethal egg exploded with a low *whump*, and the street was instantly choked with thick white smoke.

Bolan fired a burst into the smoke, then stopped. Firing blind, there was every chance that the slugs might go through the windows of apartments, killing or injuring innocent civilians. The gunman in the Mercedes wasn't as cautious. Rounds banged on the pavement and ricocheted across the street—but to no effect, as the gunman could no more see his targets than they could see him.

The Mercedes shrieked away from the curb and toward the roadblock at the south end of the street. The men crouched behind the police car opened fire. Suddenly they were thrown back by the explosions of concussion and shrapnel grenades.

The heavy luxury sedan jumped the curb and raced down the sidewalk, flattening two small trees, knocking down a telephone kiosk and scattering litter cans. Another smoke grenade was lobbed from the vehicle, blinding the policemen who were trying to stop the car with bursts of fire.

Bolan rose to his knees, took steady aim with the Desert Eagle and loosed a shot into the rear of the speeding, swerving Mercedes. The fuel tank burst with a whoosh of yellow flame, but the car sped on, fueled for another hundred yards by the gasoline in its lines and pumps, after which it coasted on its momentum. It careered around a corner and out of sight.

Slugs whining off the pavement forced Bolan to turn his attention to the men who had gotten out of the Mercedes when it was stopped. Syrkin was down, rolling and clutching his leg. Bolan could make out three men on the sidewalk in front of the apartment building. One of them pitched forward, shot from behind by one of the officers in the hallway of the apartment building. Another turned and fired a burst into that hallway, dropping at least two men.

The Executioner blasted the man who had chopped down the policemen in the hall. The cannonlike roar of the Desert Eagle filled the street, and the man with the grease gun flopped on his back.

A stream of slugs from Lemaire's MAT 49 whipped past Bolan and chewed into the legs of the third man from the Mercedes.

Then the street was silent. Syrkin groaned, and a French policeman cried out in pain. But the gunplay was over.

DAVID SYRKIN AND four wounded policemen were taken to the hospital. Hit in the upper leg, Syrkin would be out of action for a while. One of the policemen died in the emergency room.

Two men from the Mercedes were dead on the sidewalk in front of the apartment building. The third was taken to the same hospital where Syrkin and the policemen were taken, where his legs were amputated. He couldn't be readily identified; neither could one of the dead men lying on the concrete. The other dead man was Abu Vilad.

"It was Malik," Lemaire grunted. "And the woman. They got away."

"Worse than that," Bolan told him. "We have no more idea than we did before where the plutonium has gone. But it'll show up, and the world's going to regret what's going to happen."

3

Brognola had called late in the afternoon and asked Bolan to meet him at a sidewalk table at a small café on the slope of Montmartre, as fast as he could get there.

"What do you know about Majorca?" the big Fed began without preamble.

Bolan shrugged. "Mediterranean island off the Spanish coast that's usually loaded with tourists. Nice climate, never too hot or too cold, they say."

"You're about to learn a whole lot more about it. Tomorrow, every newspaper in the world will give the whole front page to Majorca. Tonight, there'll be nothing else on TV news."

"Why?"

"There's been a damned catastrophe there. Maybe a hundred dead. We wondered what terrorists would do with cesium 137. Well, now we know. I've just come from a long session with Lemaire and some others. They've been on the phone with Spain practically all day."

"What happened?" Bolan asked.

"The big town on the island is Palma. The two luxury hotels on the west end of the waterfront are called the Hotel Elisabeth and the Hotel San Francisco. That's where the trouble began—in the swimming pools."

The Executioner cocked an eyebrow.

Brognola nodded. "You want to know how bad it is? Just listen. The tragedy started about nine this morning at the Elisabeth. The pool really wasn't open yet, but one of the guests was already in the water. So the lifeguard went out and started his routine—you know, checking the water temperature and the chlorine to be sure the pool was okay for swimming. Everything seemed all right, but it sure as hell wasn't. The guest who was swimming suddenly started to vomit. He hung over the end of the pool and vomited his guts out on the brick pavement."

"Radiation sickness," Bolan said grimly.

"Right. So the lifeguard and the assistant manager ran over and helped the man out of the water. They got him into a chair, and he started to vomit blood. The hotel rules for helping sick guests are, first to help the guest in any way possible, and second to get him out of sight. So these two fellows lifted the man to his feet and took him inside. Since he looked like he was about to vomit again, they took him into the first private room available, which was the store room for dining-room linen. The lifeguard stayed with the guest while the other guy went to a phone and called for a doctor.

"Something worse happened five or ten minutes later at the San Francisco Hotel," Brognola continued. "As soon as the lifeguard went out and sat down on his chair, five kids jumped into the pool. Ten minutes later all five of them were vomiting blood, and the manager called the emergency squad."

Bolan shook his head. "Five kids . . ."

"It gets worse yet," Brognola warned as he set down his cup of café au lait. "Back over at the Elisabeth, other guests jumped into the pool, and *they* started to vomit. So another emergency squad was called."

"Cesium in the water of both those pools."

"A person didn't have to get in the swimming pool to be poisoned by the radiation," Brognola went on. "The manager and the lifeguard at the Elisabeth both collapsed. They'd put their arms around the first man and sort of half carried him, and that got enough contaminated water on them to make them sick. Both of them have died. Just from carrying the guy back to the linen room. Okay, so the hotel managers figured the pool water was contaminated and closed the pools. Then at the Elisabeth people started to get sick in the dining room."

"How'd the contamination get in there?" Bolan asked.

"They don't know for sure, but remember they carried the first man into the linen room. The contamination must have gotten on the tablecloths and napkins. One guess is that they rolled up a couple of tablecloths and put them under the sick man's head, then folded them and put them back on the shelf. Anyway, it looks like eight people may have died from contact with one or two tablecloths—people who ate at the table, plus a waitress and a busboy."

"That's hard to believe."

"That's what we're up against," Brognola replied. "That's what cesium 137 can do. Technicians have been confirming it. When the local doctors finally began to suspect the problem was radiation sickness and not bacterial infection, they screamed for help. The first help they got was a team of medical technicians from an American carrier, the *John F. Kennedy*, that's stationed in the Mediterranean. Four F-14s from the carrier landed four medics riding in the radar operators' seats. Those guys saw what the story was and got the local doctors doing the right things. Within a couple of hours other medical teams came in from all over Europe. But it was too late for a lot of people."

"How many?" Bolan asked.

"Like I said, it could be a hundred when they're all counted. Five emergency squadmen. Three doctors. Some parents, from clutching their kids to them as they were dying. The radiation from the kids' bodies killed the parents, if you can believe that."

"I believe it," Bolan said somberly.

"Besides that," Brognola went on, "the manager of the San Francisco ordered the pool drained, thinking it had a bacterial infection in it. The radioactive water ran through a pipe and into a gully, through a culvert and out into the water off the beach. Some kids that were playing in the gully are dying. Two or three kids who were playing on the beach. Some people who worked at the hotels, one way and another. People who tried to help the sick people. A man who thought he should hose down the empty swimming pool and got down in it with a hose. And so on. Hundreds sick. Maybe a hundred dead."

"Lots of people won't know for months, maybe for years, what exposure to that radiation may have done to them," Bolan added.

Brognola nodded and stared at the table for a moment.

The warrior clenched his fists, angry at the thought of terrorists who could even think of driving home a point in this way. He wondered, briefly, what kind of man could mastermind this heinous act. But almost before the thought was fully formed he had the answer—he'd been fighting men like this for a long time.

A FEW MINUTES LATER a car pulled up, and Paul Lemaire got out. He walked to their table and thrust a piece of paper toward Brognola. The Fed frowned over it for a moment, then passed it to Bolan.

It was a photocopy of a press release that had been received by the Paris newspapers, as well as newspapers all over the world.

DECLARATION OF THE PEOPLES OF THE WORLD

Let the imperialists ponder the vengeance taken on the island of Majorca. We, the United Righteous, declare our unyielding determination to terminate all forms of capitalist-imperialist domination. You have seen what we have done. You know we can do it again. And again! Prepare to surrender. The terms will be communicated. In the meantime, the murder of our comrades must cease. The cowardly attack in Paris will be avenged!

"Well, we know something," Bolan said. "The so-called United Righteous is the Islamic Strike Force—or the ISF is part of the UR. If they were really smart, they'd have kept quiet about that. I guess emotion has overpowered reason."

"Doesn't it always?" Lemaire asked sarcastically. "Here is a partial list of the dead on Majorca." He pushed that paper toward Bolan, rather than Brognola.

The list didn't give just names. It also gave nationalities and ages. "Children," the warrior said. "It doesn't make any difference to them, does it?"

"Napoleon Malik has disappeared," Lemaire told him. "Maybe he's no longer in France."

"I'm going back to the States," Bolan said. "Sooner or later this crowd will attack there."

"Or in Israel," Lemaire added.

"Or in Israel. But Israel has means to cope with it. In the United States—"

"They may need someone with unorthodox methods."

FOUR-WHEEL DRIVE almost wasn't enough on such bad roads. Brad Buckley glanced nervously at the grim, silent Japanese who sat in the passenger seat. Nothing seemed to move the man. You couldn't make conversation with him. It was as if he didn't speak English, though Brad had heard him speak it and knew he did, very well.

He was called the Shark. Brad had heard his real name but couldn't remember it. At the Holiday Inn he'd had to ask just for a Japanese, and that had been enough. The desk man had known who he meant.

The cover story was that the Shark represented a company that was interested in buying a tract of mountain land and building a resort hotel. You had to be a fool to believe that, but folks in the area did believe it. They *wanted* to believe it, would believe anything that might bring some money and maybe some jobs.

In Boone County, West Virginia, there wasn't much left. What little coal a man could grub out of the old mines could hardly be sold. There were no trains anymore, and the coal had to be hauled by truck—that is, if anybody could be found who wanted to buy it. Of course there had never been any farming to amount to anything on these mountainsides.

At one time there'd been some money in making whiskey. Brad's father and grandfather had worked in mines and ran stills, both. Now . . . people didn't like mountain whiskey anymore. If they could afford whiskey, they could afford better. A few men made some, but drank most of it themselves.

Brad figured he was lucky. He wasn't sure what these fellows were doing, but he didn't care. They were paying. As a small coal operator he couldn't make a living off his old mines, but these fellows wanted to store something underground. More than that, they wanted to do some kind of lab work down below. And they paid. Generously.

They paid with checks on a big New York bank, in the name of a company called United Resorts, Inc. The monthly checks would keep coming for a long time, he'd been told, provided he kept his mouth firmly shut.

Brad knew they were doing something illegal. Maybe the stuff they carried into the old mine shafts was cocaine. But he didn't care. Hell, he couldn't afford to care.

His mines were perfect for doing something you wanted to keep hidden. In the first place, they were remote—hell and gone from anywhere. The country store, post office and half dozen houses that comprised Rickety, West Virginia, had been abandoned ten years ago.

And rickety was what the place had been in its best days. The hills had hardly been cleared and were thick-grown with big old trees and thorny brush. Since no coal was hauled anymore, nobody bothered about the roads. The last time he'd hauled coal, he'd had to fix up a half mile of road himself. Nobody ever came up here, not even hunters.

The old mines were horizontal shafts, dug into the mountainside, not vertical shafts. A man could walk in, if he had guts. The shoring was still good, though these fellows had done a lot of work on it—fearing the shaft would fall in on them, he supposed.

They had driven up the mountain in small trucks—new ones—hauling small loads of whatever it was they were putting back inside the mine shafts. They brought maybe a ton at a time, certainly no more, and he wasn't welcome to be around when the deliveries were made.

The pickup bounced over the last hundred yards of rocky terrain and came to the big old slag piles. The stuff had been heaped there for a hundred years. When it rained, the runoff from the slag poisoned the ground down below, and the mountain slope was treeless, scarred for half a mile. Some government agents had been around three or four years ago, making noises about his having to do something about that. Brad had laughed at them, told them he sure couldn't afford to haul that slag away, nor to pay a fine for not hauling it, either; so if the government wanted it moved, the government would have to move it.

He was able to shift up into second gear as the pickup rolled into the clearing between the slag piles and the mine.

"There y'go," he said to the Japanese. "Buckley Number Three."

Isoroku Akada made a quick visual inspection of the depository. It was as it had been described, and looked satisfactory. His subordinates' vehicles were parked under the trees and out of sight from the air. Their equipment was back in the shaft, far enough inside to be out of sight to someone wandering into the clearing.

He was a careful man. Back in his motel room he'd left a rolled-up set of blueprints, ostensibly plans for a resort hotel. He suspected that some West Virginian would enter his room and look at those plans while he was away.

He was a careful man in other ways. Two men kept constant watch on Buckley's eight-year-old daughter. They carried a tiny radio signal receiver. If Buckley became any kind of problem, a signal could be transmitted instantly. It was only a beep in the receiver, but it was the command to grab the child. A two-beep return signal meant she had been grabbed, and they could deal with Buckley accordingly.

"You will wait for me, Mr. Buckley," Akada instructed as he opened the door and stepped down from the truck.

Brad Buckley had heard that firm, calm tone of command in one or two voices before. He didn't like taking orders; he never had. But this time, he knew he would wait. As long as the man wanted.

"MY NAME IS Aleksandr Savacheva. Like many with that name, I am called Shondor. You may call me what you wish. My preference is Shondor."

Bolan nodded. He suspected that most people called this man whatever he wanted to be called. Shondor Savacheva was a mass of hard muscle, which was evident even through his gray tweed jacket and black slacks. His face was square and hard, and his hair was bristly, short and blond. Yet there was about this rugged man an air of joy with life. Something in his manner suggested that he was always looking for the amusing.

Savacheva had been waiting at Kennedy International Airport when Bolan arrived. A box containing the weapons Bolan had carried to France had come through as a diplomatic container and had been recovered by Shondor before Bolan came through passport control—as Colonel Rance Pollock—and emerged through the regular passenger checks, carrying only clothes and toiletries in his luggage.

"You can trust this man absolutely," Brognola had said when he asked Bolan to accept Savacheva as a co-worker in the battle against the United Righteous. "If we have to work with local police forces, he can handle that element, and we might have to call for that kind of help."

"Understood," Bolan had replied.

Shondor picked up Bolan's suitcase and strode toward the exit before the Executioner could object. He had a car in the short-term parking lot. Bolan's box was already in the trunk.

"You hungry?" Shondor asked. "You need to go to the bathroom? We have a long drive ahead of us."

"Where are we going?"

Shondor cranked the steering wheel around and headed the Ford toward the exit from the parking lot. "Pittsburgh," he said. "Columbus. Indianapolis. Saint Louis. You can sleep. Maybe I'll ask you to drive later."

"Why aren't we flying?"

"We will stop and call Washington from time to time. We may be diverted."

"LADIES AND GENTLEMEN—"

The President of the United States didn't wait for the completion of his introduction. He walked into the Oval Office and strode toward his desk, gesturing to the men and women assembled that they should sit down. Present were some of the most powerful people in the government: The secretary of state and the secretary of defense; the chairman of the Joint Chiefs and the director of Central Intelligence; the attorney general, the director of the Federal Bureau of Investigation and the director of Sensitive Operations Group, Department of Justice; the majority and minority leaders, United States Senate; the Speaker of the House of Representatives and the minority leader of the House.

"I had hoped this meeting could be smaller," the President began, "but everyone here is entitled to the information we have and to take part in the discussion. We face a threat, and we have major decisions to make."

The people seated on the chairs and couches stared at the grim face of the President, then glanced at one another. They had been summoned from their dinners, some actually from their beds, to come to this meeting. They knew it was important; they had understood that before they arrived here.

"I will read to you the message we have received from a group that chooses to call itself the United Righteous," the President said. "The name itself suggests what kind of people we are dealing with. Here's what it says."

He unfolded a paper, put on his reading glasses and read the message aloud.

"We the people, determined no longer to tolerate American and other criminal-imperialist aggressions, have acquired the means of enforcing our just will. To display our new power, we arranged the Majorca incident, which everyone knowledgeable about this kind of power will understand was but a minor demonstration. The great criminals possess the big bomb. We possess the poor man's 'bomb,' which, let it be understood, is at least as powerful as the bombs used to subdue the righteous, anti-imperialist Japanese people in 1945.

"A little cesium in two swimming pools—and death! Multiply that by ten thousand, by a hundred thousand, and introduce it into the water of— What water? We will choose.

"Where? When? Where and when we shall decide.

"These are our initial demands. Others will follow. To avoid the effects of our righteous indignation, the great criminals will:

(1) Immediately withdraw all United States naval and military forces from the Mediterranean Sea and all lands bordering on that water, as well as from the Indian Ocean, the Persian Gulf and all lands bordering on them.

(2) Withdraw all Zionist aliens from every hectare of land invaded and stolen by the Zionists since 1948.

(3) Withdraw all British criminal occupiers from Ireland.

(4) Liberate all freedom fighters from prisons. A list of such men and women will be issued shortly.

"These are our initial demands. To avoid another demonstration of our power, the criminal imperialists will give evidence of their acceptance of our terms by making major progress toward meeting these initial demands. Immediately.

"The people of the world are watching! We can be deceived no longer! We will tolerate no longer! The alternative is death."

"Something similar was delivered to the president of France and the British prime minister," the President concluded wearily.

"They grabbed another truck of nuclear waste in southern Ohio this afternoon," the secretary of defense added. "Waste. Not fissionable. Just dirty radioactive sludge, the same kind of stuff that was taken in South Carolina and Kentucky."

"Why the hell can't that stuff be protected?" the President demanded angrily. "The pattern is clear enough. We know what they're doing. The Italians lost some more cesium today. If we know what they want to steal, why can't we stop them?"

"There's too much of the stuff, Mr. President," the director of the FBI said, "too widely dispersed. The truck in Ohio was guarded by the state highway patrol and two of my agents, heavily armed." He shrugged. "They were hit hard, by men with automatic weapons."

"We can't put troops on every shipment of nuclear waste from every nuclear power plant in the Unites States," the secretary of defense stated.

"The hell you can't! Your job is to defend the country. So defend it against this."

"There must be ten thousand installations in this country alone where radioactive material is used for one purpose or another," said the director of the CIA. "Laboratories, hospitals, clinics, industrial plants..."

The President looked around the Oval Office, gazing momentarily into the eyes of every man and woman. The anger faded from his face. "All right," he said quietly. "Does anyone propose that we surrender?"

He waited. No one spoke. Then the attorney general shook his head. The Senate minority leader shook her head, as did the others.

"All right," the President said. "We know what we have to do. I want this so-called United Righteous organization identified. I want its members tracked down and neutralized. And quick. No niceties." He looked at the directors of the FBI and CIA, then at the attorney general and Brognola. "I'll take the flack. If anyone here objects to a dirty fight, no holds barred, speak now."

"Or forever hold your peace," the attorney general muttered.

SAVACHEVA PLACED a call to Washington at a gas station on the Pennsylvania Turnpike. He came back to the car with word of the attack on the shipment of nuclear waste in southern Ohio. They drove on and stopped again in Columbus, Ohio. They might as well take a couple of rooms and spend the night there, Shondor stated after he reported to Bolan the results of a couple of calls. They might as well have dinner and get a night's sleep. Everyone else was— everyone, that is, that they might want to talk to around Piketon, Ohio.

"We have an identity or two," Shondor said as they sat down to dinner. He had spoken to a contact at Justice just before he sat down. "I don't know how we know this. The thing is, of course, on a need-to-know basis. I'd guess we have a mole in Tripoli."

"Let's don't speculate."

Shondor nodded. "Abu Vilad was in Sidi just before he died, where he met with General Laqiya. He met, not only with the mad general, but with a group of other men. Two of them were Isoroku Akada and Albrecht Kirchner."

"I've heard of them," Bolan replied. "Kirchner is one of the survivors of the Baader-Meinhof gang. As for Akada, I always thought he was behind the Red Sun operations, though he wasn't there for the shootout. Vilad, Kirchner, Akada . . . three bad cats."

"There were others at the meeting," Shondor continued. "Our source seems to like to release information in dribbles."

"As the money dribbles in," Bolan said dryly.

"I suppose so. Anyway, who would be the American in this group?"

Bolan shook his head. "There wouldn't necessarily be one. If there is, he's a mercenary."

"Major Stamford?"

Bolan shrugged. "He'd fit in with that crowd."

"Well, I was thinking about why they would have hijacked a truck going out of this Ohio nuclear power plant. Why southern Ohio? I can think of two reasons—first, that they are planning their next demonstration for somewhere in this area, and second, that somebody is working on his home turf. Stamford was born and reared in Parkersburg, West Virginia."

"Speculation."

"He's also missing," Shondor pressed. "I asked for a check on him. He's missing from his place in Palm Beach. His boat is there. His girlfriend is there. The major is not there."

"We'll keep it in mind."

4

As they drove south along the Scioto River, they left the rich, flat farm country of central Ohio and entered the hill country, part of what was once called Appalachia.

"Dirt poor," Shondor observed.

Mack Bolan didn't respond to the comment. His mind was fixed on something else, something Shondor had said last night. There were many atomic power plants in the States. Every one of them produced hazardous radioactive waste that had to be hauled somewhere and somehow disposed of. The material was bulky, heavy and dangerous to handle. What was more, it was difficult to disguise as you drove along the highways with it. So, if you were going to steal the stuff, you'd steal it where you were going to use it. Or not far away.

It didn't make sense any other way. So what could they have in mind to do with it here?

He scanned the highway map from the glove compartment of the car. Okay, looking at the Ohio River: Cincinnati, Louisville. A little north: Columbus, Dayton. On west: Indianapolis, Saint Louis. The heartland. The rustbelt. The urban heartland of America, where the nation could be damaged.

"Portsmouth," Shondor announced as they passed into a town where the Scioto River flowed into the Ohio.

The Ohio Highway Patrol wasn't big about high-sounding titles of rank. A sergeant met them at the little brick headquarters building they called a barracks. He was a Smoky, in uniform of gray and black, with a tall campaign hat. His name was Mulligan, and he was humorless.

He had reason to be. "I spent most of last night, me and my wife, with the pretty little girl that was married to the man killed yesterday," he said. "That is, except when I was at the hospital with the family of the man who was wounded. That's why I wasn't available for calls from Washington. Or Columbus, either."

"It's the frontline troops who always get it," Bolan commented.

"You know something about that, do you?" Sergeant Mulligan asked.

Shondor answered. "Colonel Pollock has been in the front line in every sense of the term. Combat in Vietnam, the war against terrorism. He's got scars to prove it. As do I, for that matter."

Mulligan sighed. "Sorry, gentlemen. It's been a tough twenty-four hours."

Bolan walked to the window of the little building and looked out at the hills of southern Ohio, where the leaves were beginning to turn, and a fog like England's lay over the valleys.

"They hit you with heavy weapons?" he asked.

Sergeant Mulligan nodded. "I got boys here from the FBI and from the BCI—that's the Ohio Bureau of Criminal Identification. The 9 mm stuff came in like water out of fire hoses. Nobody had a chance. Besides my boys, the FBI lost a man. Plus the truck driver was killed."

The sergeant sighed again. "What the hell are they gonna do with that stuff? I mean, you can't make bombs with it. This stuff was just sludge, so to speak, on its way out to

Utah to be poured down in some kind of mine, as I get it. And deadly. What the hell are they gonna do with it?''

Bolan answered, "When we catch up with them, we'll find out."

"Okay. Let's get down to business. They took the truck. It's kind of a tank truck, lead-lined. We found that on a country road, half a dozen miles from no place, with most of the stuff pumped out of it. That means two things, if you don't mind my saying so. It means somebody either knew what he was doing or is dead by now from the radiation. It also means somebody knew where he was going, 'cause there aren't many places you could go to transfer that stuff from one vehicle to another and not be seen doing it.''

"A local, you think?" Shondor asked.

Mulligan nodded. "People around here know the schedule for hauling radioactive waste, and they know the route. They picked a good place for their attack. Then somebody knew where to go.''

"A local would have no use for that hot sludge," Bolan said. "So he was working for somebody else, for money.''

"Well, there's people around here can use money," Mulligan agreed. "You've seen more prosperous communities.''

"Summarizing," Shondor said, "nobody saw the truck or trucks the stuff was pumped into, so nobody can guess which way the terrorists went with it, right?''

"Well, sort of," the sergeant agreed. "But not exactly. We figured it had to be some kind of tank truck, which is what the stuff was taken from, so we got out a bulletin to watch for tank trucks. You can always miss. The truck could have been disguised. But we had roadblocks on the main roads from half an hour after the attack, and figure it took at least that long to transfer the stuff to the different truck.''

"So?"

"We covered Route 23, north and south. Everything that looked like a tank truck was stopped. Unless they someway missed, the stuff didn't go up 23 to Columbus. And it didn't go across 32, either, to Cincinnati or east to where 32 intersects U.S. 50."

"Lead-lined tank inside an ordinary semitrailer," Bolan suggested.

"Nope. Thought of that, too. Stopped every one of them. So the stuff went out of Scioto County on a country road."

"Which tells us what?" Bolan probed, sure that it did tell this man something.

"It tells us the stuff went in more than one truck, to start with. Roads they had to use wouldn't take a big taker or a heavy semi. Bridges wouldn't take the weight. And we got sheriffs' deputies in these counties that watch those bridges damned close, which our killers must know, since they know so much about things around here. The amount of radioactive sludge that was in that tanker had to go into two smaller trucks, maybe three or four. And, well, that's what I figure, unless I'm all the way off base."

SERGEANT MULLIGAN couldn't have imagined how very much on base he was.

The lead-lined tanks were rectangular, roughly four feet wide by six long and three deep. They were built into the beds of fifteen pickup trucks fitted with camper bodies. The weight was carried by reinforced chassis and suspensions. Two other trucks were pumpers, equipped to transfer materials from big tankers into the small tanks in the pickups. The pumps and crews were highly efficient and could fill one of the small lead-lined tanks in less than three minutes. Two more trucks carried water tanks and high-pressure pumps and hoses used to spray down each newly loaded truck and wash away any trace of radioactivity that might have gotten loose during the transfer.

While the small trucks were still wet from the hoses, men shoveled dust or mud over them. They bore West Virginia, Kentucky and Tennessee license plates, and the men who drove them wore green or khaki work clothes or hunting clothes. They carried shotguns and fishing equipment. They also carried heavier weapons, concealed in special compartments built into the trucks.

The destination for the fleet of little trucks was Brad Buckley's mine in Boone County, West Virginia. They crossed the Ohio River on bridges as far apart as Maysville, Kentucky and Saint Marys, West Virginia, avoiding the main highways and making their way slowly across winding country roads that eventually converged on Boone County.

It was the rule that no more than two trucks appeared at the mine at the same time, and no more than four in one day. Some of the drivers stayed in motels in small towns in Ohio, Kentucky and West Virginia, waiting for their appointed time to drive up Buckley's road and into the clearing between the slag heap and the mine shaft.

When Bolan and Savacheva were talking with Sergeant Mulligan, one of the trucks carrying radioactive sludge was parked at a Holiday Inn just outside Ironton, Ohio, where its driver and guard had spent the night. They slept late. They had only a short drive that day, to Logan, West Virginia, where they would stay overnight in another Holiday Inn and drive on the next day to Logan County and the Buckley mine.

ISOROKU AKADA sat in a luxurious room in the Greenbrier Hotel at White Sulphur Springs, West Virginia. Ostensibly he had come to play golf, and he had brought his clubs and fully meant to be out on the course a little after noon.

"I guess the general pays well," Major Isaac Stamford commented.

The Shark looked up from his room service breakfast of bacon, eggs, toast and coffee. "General Laqiya pays nothing," he stated firmly. "I do not work for him. Neither do you."

"It's his money. There's an old American saying—'He who pays the piper calls the tune.'"

Akada shook his head irritably. "Major Stamford, if it is your impression that General Laqiya calls the tune, then I might have no further use for you. *I* call your tune, Major. Let there be no mistake about that."

Major Stamford fixed calm, appraising eyes on the Japanese for a long moment. Then he shrugged and said, "Okay. I'm glad to have it clarified."

Major Stamford was a bald man with a small round face and indistinct gray eyes. He was forty-four years old. Dishonorably discharged from the United States Marines, he had served four years in Leavenworth for systematic and cleverly concealed embezzlement of government funds over a period of eighteen months. He was caught only two or three fund transfers short of his planned disappearance to Brazil.

"I, too," said the Shark, "am glad to have the matter clarified. You will be well paid for your contribution to our—"

"Half a million, I believe we agreed on," the major interrupted.

Akada nodded. "At least. Maybe more. But you will receive half a million dollars, American. From me, Major Stamford. General Laqiya is providing the money, but you will receive it from me. The general never heard of you."

"The money's in hand?"

The Shark smiled. "Yes. It is in hand. I don't trust him, either."

Major Stamford reached for the pot and poured himself a cup of coffee. "We're not far from being ready."

"We will require the second set of trucks. The big ones."

"They're being built in a shop just outside of Parkersburg," Stamford informed him. "We could work faster except for the lead. There's a hell of a lot of nervousness about lead these days. There's nervousness about missing radioactive material and how it's being moved. You order a big shipment of lead, you're asked tough questions."

"What are you doing about it?"

"We're stealing it," Stamford replied.

"Where? How?"

"Everywhere. All over. A little bit at a time. It's not a precious metal, so stocks of it aren't guarded. We can pick up a ton of it without anybody noticing it's missing. That is, they won't notice for a while."

"This must be done carefully," the Shark warned.

"It's *being* done carefully."

"I want to review the plan. I want to have it firmly fixed in my mind. Describe for me again what happened after the oil spill."

Stamford nodded. "Okay. A few years ago there was a major oil spill just upstream from Pittsburgh. A big tank ruptured on the banks of the Monongahela River and spilled something like three-quarters of a million gallons of diesel fuel into the river. The oil moved slowly downstream on the current and into the Ohio River. It passed Pittsburgh in two or three days, Wheeling, West Virginia, after about a week, then on down the Ohio. Cities as far downstream as Cincinnati and Louisville had to close their water intake valves and draw their municipal water from sources other than the river. Now—"

The Shark grinned. "Now, if that oil spill had been radioactive..."

"Right. If the spill had been radioactive."

"I am not sure it will kill a very large number of people," the Shark said. "A few hundred, a few thousand. But the *panic*!"

"Right. Americans don't know how to cope with panic."

"Very well." Akada had finished with his breakfast, though he left half of it on his plate. He rose and walked to the window, looking out at the changing leaves on the nearby mountains. "We will not have three-quarters of a million gallons."

"We don't need three-quarters of a million gallons," Stamford told him. "The trucks we're getting ready can carry 7,500 gallons each. Ten of them can carry 75,000 gallons. That's not 75,000 gallons of diesel oil but 75,000 of radioactive sludge—mixed with oil to keep it from dissipating too fast in the river. Hey—" he shook his head and smiled "—a man could survive if he got a few drops of diesel oil in his drinking water, but—"

"But not if he gets a tiny quantity of radioactive sludge."

"There's some really good stuff in that sludge," the major said. "Strontium 90, plutonium, mercury. Some of that stuff's going to settle into the riverbeds, and those rivers are going to be hot for years. Plus the oil you're mixing in. That's going to be radioactive, too. And it'll float. How's the mixing coming? Anybody getting sick?"

The Shark nodded. "Two men. We had to shoot them."

"Yes. You had to shoot them. So where does the sludge go? I need to look for the place where we dump it in the water."

"I have been studying the maps," the Shark said. "I would like to carry the material up to the headwaters of the Monongahela River and let it flow down past Pittsburgh, but I am afraid that's too long a journey for our radioactive sludge. A lot of it would remain in woodland streams. Besides, it might take two weeks to reach Pittsburgh, by which time the city could be well prepared. I am afraid we have to think in terms of the Kanawha River."

"The Guyandot," Stamford suggested.

"Guyandot..." the Shark muttered, peering at his map.

"It would reach Huntington within twelve hours. That's a town of 65,000 roughly. The stuff might get there before anyone identified it. It might get sucked into their municipal water system."

"I see it." Akada put a finger on the map. "Into the Ohio River at Huntington."

"It would reach Cincinnati in about a week," the major said. "Another week, or a little less, Louisville. Anyway, 200 miles of the Ohio Valley will be in panic. River traffic will stop. You know what they carry on the river? Coal. Oil. Gasoline. Limestone. Sulfur. Industries will shut down. Some towns will have to be evacuated. They'll be afraid to drink the water, and they'll be afraid of the river."

"Afraid of the river," Akada repeated, smiling. "Yes. And many will die. Thousands, I should think. Others will be made ill. Tens of thousands. So, confusion and fear. Yes. Perfect."

Major Stamford's thoughts had returned to a mental calculation he had been making. "With the trucks we're building, we can dump 75,000 gallons of sludge into the Guyandot River. And since we only have to move it forty miles or so from the mine to the dump site, we might be able to return for a second load and bring it to the river before anyone finds out what's happening."

"Find two dump sites, Major," the Shark ordered. "One nearer, one farther. We will use the farther one first, then the nearer one. Then we abandon everything. We'll have put in the little river as much as 150,000 gallons of radioactive sludge mixed with oil."

"That should make quite a demonstration. They'll take us very seriously after that."

MACK BOLAN WAS studying an enhanced satellite photo of southeastern Ohio, northeastern West Virginia and a bit of northern Kentucky.

"There could be ten thousand places in this area where they could haul that stuff and hide it," he said.

"Where would you put it?" Sergeant Mulligan asked. "Where in hell would you store radioactive waste?"

"In an abandoned mine," Bolan replied.

The sergeant nodded. "There could be ten thousand of those."

"There would be records," Shondor said, "federal and state records—what mines are being worked, which are abandoned."

"That still leaves ten thousand," the sergeant said gloomily.

"Lead," Bolan said abruptly.

"What?"

"Lead. The hijacked tanker was lead-lined, to contain the radiation."

"Which made it one hell of a heavy truck," Mulligan commented.

"Right. And if the radioactive waste was carried away in smaller trucks, they had to be lead-lined. What's more, if the stuff is being stored in abandoned mines, there have to be lead-lined tanks in those mines. They're not just pouring the stuff down mine shafts. They want to get it out again sooner or later, so they have to be pumping it into tanks.''

"So who's buying lead, huh?''

"Make a call to Washington, Shondor. Tell them to find out who sells industrial quantities of lead in this area. Then have them call those suppliers and find out if they have any big new customers."

"Another idea,'' Sergeant Mulligan said. He began to shuffle papers on his desk. "Let me see here...these reports. Okay. Here. Theft of lead ingots. Plant down the river from Marietta. And here's another one. Industrial supply yard outside Jackson. Lead pipe. Let's see. They took about a ton of ingots. And pipe...two hundred feet of two-inch. That's a lot of pipe. I mean, that'd be heavy."

"Okay,'' Bolan said. "So they're not buying it. They're stealing it.''

"This is a hell of a big operation, gentlemen.''

Bolan frowned. "It involves too many people.''

JIM FARRELL, working in the mine, knew he was doomed. He could feel the symptoms. He'd guessed he was working with radioactive sludge, and he knew he was being exposed to the radiation. He felt more and more nauseous. He'd seen others being allowed to crawl away, retching. They had never returned to the work.

Escape. It was all he had thought of at first, but his legs were chained together. There was only one way out of the mine—shot dead by the ugly little automatic weapons toted by the guards. After he gave up on escape, he'd thought about survival. But, now all he thought about was dying, about how soon it would be and how much it would hurt.

He had begun to understand what they were doing. The radioactive material was pumped from trucks out at the mine entrance, into tank carts that rolled on rails. He and the other naked workmen dragged the carts back into the shaft more than a hundred yards. The shaft branched there, and in branch tunnels were big covered lead vats set in pits that they'd dug in the floor. The stuff ran out of the carts and into the vats.

Then diesel fuel and used crankcase oil—dirty, gummy stuff—was poured in and stirred. What was being made was a sticky, violently poisonous mess.

The vats and the tanks on the carts were lined with lead, but the workmen were exposed to radiation whenever the hatches were opened, particularly for the stirring; and the rake handles used for stirring weren't long enough to distance a man enough from the radiation. Sooner or later every man and woman who worked in the shaft would die.

The women did the lighter work. They carried food and water to the workmen; they carried away and emptied the slop buckets; they helped the sick. One of them, called Beth, spent most of her time on the lights—that is, on the crude old wiring and bare bulbs. They were barely clothed and chained, as were the men.

Every man and woman who worked in the mine was a wanted criminal. Farrell, with four others, had been helped to escape from a station wagon carrying them to the penitentiary. Some escape.

His links between his handcuffs and leg irons had been severed, but his ''liberators'' had locked on their own chains. He still wore the jail cuffs and leg irons, though they weren't hooked together.

Beth, the only one of the women he'd gotten to know, still wore a cuff, just one, locked around her right wrist. She'd been handcuffed to another woman. She'd told him she was on her way to do five years for armed robbery when she was—as she put it—kidnapped.

Kidnapped. That was a better word for it.

Beth understood as much as he did, and she was resigned to it. Some understood and weren't resigned. But only two men had been shot. One had been whipped. And all of them were going to die.

"BINGO." Shondor put down the telephone. "The FBI says the sheriff of Pleasants County, West Virginia, is holding a pair of lead thieves."

"Can we get a chopper?" Bolan asked. "I've got a feeling we don't have much time."

A little more than an hour later an Ohio Highway Patrol helicopter landed on the high school football field at Saint Marys, West Virginia. Bolan and Savacheva were met by the sheriff, a tall, long-faced man named Ed Higgins. He drove them to his office, which was in a white frame house, and led them back to the small, square, cinder-block building that was the county jail.

The jail consisted of four tiny cells in a row. A ragged, bearded man was asleep in one of them. In another cell a man in his twenties sat dejectedly on his chain-hung bunk. In the third, a woman of about the same age stood clutching the bars and glaring angrily at the sheriff.

"Meet the Clendenins," the sheriff announced. "Luke and Betsy. Thieves. Steal anything that ain't nailed down. Caught 'em one time with a cow they'd took. Judge let 'em off on that one."

"After we'd already been in jail five months," Betsy sneered sullenly. "Some lettin' off!"

"Well, anyways, this time they loaded their pickup with bars of lead they got by bustin' through the fence at the refinery."

"Never busted no fence," Luke muttered. "It was busted through already. Figured them bars was just junk they'd left layin' on the ground."

"And you put so many of 'em on your truck that you busted the springs." The sheriff laughed. "They were on their way down Route 2, and that truck settled down like an old pig settlin' down to wallow."

"Where were you taking the lead?" Shondor asked.

"Who's askin'?"

It was the young woman who spoke for the pair. She was a mannish creature except for her prominent breasts. Her blond hair was cut short, and she wore a man's checkered shirt and blue jeans. She curled her arm around one of the bars of her cell door, tipped her head to one side and fixed a challenging stare, first on Shondor, then on Bolan.

"Federal officers," the sheriff told her, "interested in who's buyin' lead."

Bolan stepped close to her and said quietly, "How'd you like to get out of here, charges dropped?"

"Wait a minute!" the sheriff protested.

"We can make it good, Sheriff," Shondor said. "Explanation later."

THE CLENDENIN PICKUP was beyond repair, so Bolan drove another one that night—a wheezing old wreck with rusted-out fenders that flapped and threatened to fall off as the long-gone shocks failed to absorb the jolts from the road. Shondor followed in a rented Chevrolet, with Sheriff Higgins riding with him.

Betsy sat beside Bolan. She'd insisted she didn't know the name of the place where she and her husband had meant to take the lead, but she knew how to get there. She could show them the place.

The sheriff had sworn Betsy was likely to jump out and run if she got the chance, even if Luke did remain behind in jail, and he'd insisted on handcuffing her, which, to Bolan's surprise, didn't bother Betsy in the least. She had offered her wrists without a word and wore the cuffs with no apparent discomfort or embarrassment.

A part of the price of her cooperation had been a carton of cigarettes, and she smoked one after another as they drove toward Parkersburg. The stink of cigarette smoke was perhaps a blessing, Bolan decided, since once the doors were closed it became all too apparent that Betsy hadn't had a bath since she was in jail, and maybe for two weeks before that.

"Fed, huh?" she said. "Not FBI, though. Right? You ain't explained why you take so much interest in that there lead."

"None of your business," Bolan replied. "If it gets you out of jail, that's good enough."

She shrugged.

Betsy and Luke had explained in the jail that word had come to them from one of their friends that a shop in P-burg, as they called it, was looking for lead. They'd pay a good price and no questions asked. In fact, they'd pay a bonus for a nice load of clean lead bars.

"Anybody figures out it was us that told you 'bout this..." She stopped and shook her head. "You promised—"

"Don't worry. We'll keep our mouths shut if you keep yours shut."

"Yeah."

"How many loads of lead have you sold to this outfit?"

"I never said we sold none before."

"How many loads?"

"Just one."

"So you're sure you know where you're going."

Betsy nodded. "I know where I'm goin'."

She pointed the way, and he drove the battered pickup through Parkersburg, an unimpressive town of about forty thousand. They drove out the east side of the town on a narrow, bumpy state highway with red mud for shoulders. The surrounding country was hilly, covered with scrubby second-growth pine; and on the steep hillsides to both sides of the road stood houses, house trailers, an occasional little store, a few taverns and some auto-repair shops and junkyards.

Betsy pointed to the right, and the Executioner turned into an even narrower country road.

"The place is just ahead. Why don't you drive by and come back? That way, you get a look."

A wooden sign on the roof identified the business:

BLENNERHASSET TRUCK REPAIRS
Engines-Transmissions-Bodies
Rigs Reconditioned or Rebuilt

Though the building was made out of cinderblocks, it was no small shop. The structure was roomy enough to take at least two semitrailers inside, through wide sliding doors on the north side. Half a dozen semis were parked outside, most of them in back in various stages of repair. Half a dozen cars were parked in front. Everything—building, trucks, cars, even the littered ground—was dingy and dilapidated.

Lights shone in the windows. Apparently they were working inside.

Bolan drove on a hundred yards, then pulled to the side of the road. Shondor and the sheriff stopped behind the pickup, and they got out.

"She says that's the place," Bolan told them. "I guess we go in and take a look."

"Is it a federal offense to buy stolen lead?" Sheriff Higgins asked.

"It is in this case," Shondor replied. "You and Betsy had better stay here. Colonel Pollock and I will go in."

The sheriff shrugged. "This is Wood County," he said. "Outside my jurisdiction."

Shondor walked back to the Chevrolet and opened the trunk, returning with a pair of Uzis and holstered pistols—including Bolan's .44 Magnum Desert Eagle.

"Hey! You guys mean business!"

Bolan and Shondor walked down the dark road toward Blennerhasset Truck Repairs, talking in low voices.

"A perfect setup for putting lead-lined tanks in trucks," Shondor said. "Since they work on trucks here all the time, nobody would notice."

"Except for their buying stolen lead."

When they were within twenty yards of the building, Bolan dropped into a crouch, Shondor following suit beside him. They peered into the dim light thrown by a couple of small bulbs burning in rusty old fixtures on the outside of the building.

"Cover me," Bolan said.

He trotted forward, still in a crouch. In a moment he was pressed against the cinderblock wall of the south end of the building. He slipped along the wall to a window and risked a quick look in.

The shop was brightly lighted inside, but no work was being done. There were no trucks, and he couldn't see any workmen. He motioned Shondor forward. He, too, stared through the dirty glass of the window.

"Six cars . . . all the lights on . . . where *is* everybody?"

"Have to go in," the warrior told him.

They circled the building to the rear. The big trucks parked behind loomed in the far reaches of the light. If no one was inside, someone could be in those trucks . . . watching. Even so, they walked along the rear of the building, keeping the muzzles of the Uzis pointed toward the trucks, ready to let loose if fired on.

A flimsy wooden door was the only entrance on this side of the building. When Bolan tried it, the door swung open easily, unlocked. No reaction from inside. He and his companion quickly entered.

They stood with their backs to the rear wall, scanning their surroundings. The big shop was silent.

The machine shop was well-equipped. Two huge hoists were capable of lifting a heavy engine and moving it to a bench. There was a lathe, several big drill presses, two electric welders, acetylene torches, electric equipment for doing engine tests and sundry other pieces of equipment. Shondor pointed at a stack of lead ingots piled in the middle of the shop floor next to a furnace for melting them.

Bolan had spotted something else and jerked a thumb at that.

A man's hand, on the floor, was just visible beyond the edge of an array of oil drums.

Shondor stood alert, Uzi up and ready, while Bolan walked over to the drums.

The man on the floor was dead. He'd been shot. And behind him lay another man, also shot. They found four bodies in the machine shop.

"I'll make you a bet," Bolan said grimly. "I bet not one of those trucks out there has a lead-lined tank in it. These men finished the job, and the trucks with the tanks were driven away. Then somebody shot the mechanics because they didn't need them anymore."

Bolan glanced around the shop floor, wondering why the lights had been left on and why the bodies had been left lying there. As soon as word got out that six men had been murdered, the place would become familiar to every television viewer in America. Surely the murderers wanted to avoid that as long as possible. Didn't they?

A single shot rang out.

"Get down, Shondor!" Bolan yelled. "That's a warning from the sheriff!"

It had warned others, too. Several men kicked open the front door and rushed in, two of them carrying Uzis. Bolan and Shondor were behind cover, hidden from sight by the big lathe.

The big doors at the north end slid back, pushed by two more men, and a big yellow Ryder van backed into the machine shop.

The big doors were slid shut, and the driver climbed out of the vehicles. He was short and bald, older and very different than the other four. He wore a Colt .45 hung on a khaki web belt.

"Calm down, Homma," he barked at one of the men brandishing weapons at the door. "People shoot off guns around here. No big deal."

The man called Homma was Oriental, and the other appeared to be an Arab. The two men near the sliding door were Caucasian.

"Spread that canvas over the floor of the truck. I don't want any blood on there. Understand? And let's get the bodies over here. Homma, you pour gasoline on the bloodstains, then scrub them with that push broom. Any that don't disappear, we'll pour a little oil on. Let's get moving."

Shondor nudged Bolan and put his mouth to his ear. "Major Stamford," he whispered.

Three men dragged bodies to the truck and heaved them up inside the van. Homma, with his Uzi slung on a strap over his shoulder, splashed gasoline on one bloodstain after another and scrubbed at them with the broom.

"Let's try to take them alive," Bolan whispered. "Especially Major Stamford. I have a few questions for him."

The heavy steel body of the lathe provided a bulletproof shield for Bolan and Shondor. They rose to their feet, but kept their knees bent so that only their heads and shoulders showed above the lathe.

The Executioner squeezed off a short burst that went through the roof.

"Guns down! Hands up!" he yelled.

"Federal officers!" Shondor yelled. "You're under arrest!"

Homma refused to comply. He raised the muzzle of his Uzi and loosed a steady stream of slugs at the lathe. They ricocheted and whined away in all directions. Neither man was hit, but they had to duck down for an instant, and in that instant the Arab opened fire, too.

Seeing that his enemies were pinned, Stamford ordered his two Americans to work their way around behind some oil drums and equipment to a place where they would be angled to fire behind the lathe.

Bolan put down his Uzi and drew the Desert Eagle. He crawled to one end of the lathe and risked a quick look.

Homma stood beside the door. The Arab had taken up a position by the van and was edging his way along the wall, moving in. He'd be dangerous in a minute.

"Cover," Bolan whispered to Shondor.

Shondor held his Uzi above the body of the lathe and fired two short bursts. Homma threw himself to the floor to avoid the wild stream of slugs, and the Arab fired a burst toward the lathe before Shondor turned the Uzi toward him. Then he ducked behind a welder.

Bolan stood. In the instant that the Arab raised his head to have a look, the warrior aimed the Desert Eagle and blew away half the man's head.

Bolan dropped to cover behind the lathe before Homma could fire another burst.

"Same drill," he muttered.

Shondor nodded and raised the Uzi above his head to fire another unaimed burst in the general direction of the Japanese. The roar of the Uzi was punctuated at the end of the burst by a sharp single crack. Bolan jumped up to fire on Homma, only to see him sink to his knees, then topple forward, shot in the back by a bullet that had shattered the glass in the front door of the machine shop.

One of the Americans got off a shot with a revolver. The slug whizzed past Bolan's right arm, missing by inches. Excitement spoiled men's aim; the warrior had seen it happen many times. But it didn't spoil his. He turned the Desert Eagle toward the man who was now adjusting his aim with trembling hands. A .44 Magnum slug split the man's chest, destroying vital organs with one devastating shock.

Stamford had clambered into the van and started the engine. Now the vehicle shot forward, crashing into the closed sliding doors. The doors broke but didn't fall. The van shrieked backward, then lunged forward again. This time the doors did fall, and the vehicle bumped over them and out of the machine shop.

Bolan wanted Major Stamford alive, but he didn't intend to let him escape. He leveled the Desert Eagle on the rear of the van and fired for a tire. The big bullet didn't just blow a tire—it broke the wheel, and the van tipped to a crazy angle and stopped.

"Hey! I give up! Give up!" A revolver flew out from behind a stack of crates and skidded across the floor.

"Don't shoot! I give up! I give up!"

Bolan raced for the front door. Jerking it open, he almost ran into Sheriff Higgins, who stood on the threshold with Betsy Clendenin.

"Glad to see you alive. Do you a favor there, did I?"

Bolan nodded. "You sure did. But the leader is still loose. He was trying to drive away in the van. Now..."

"He's not leavin' in any of the cars outside," said Sheriff Higgins. "Figured somebody might try, so Betsy and I've been lettin' the air out of their tires."

Betsy, still securely handcuffed, grinned at Bolan. "You're some kind of guy, ain't ya?"

The warrior searched the darkness, looking for Stamford. He wanted him, for sure; but the guy was also capable of firing on them from the shadows.

"Get down, you two," he said. "It isn't over. A murderer is out there with a gun."

Shondor joined them, leading the man who had surrendered. "Where's the major?" he asked.

"I'd like to know," Bolan replied. "You have any more handcuffs, Sheriff? This guy needs a set. And a cell."

Bolan and Shondor began to check the vehicles in front of the machine shop—the cars belonging to the six dead men whose bodies lay in the back of the yellow van.

A shot rang out a hundred yards away, and it was plain what had happened. Major Stamford had run up the road to where Bolan and the sheriff had left the old pickup and the rented Chevrolet. He was escaping in the Chevrolet and had just put a shot through one of the tires of the pickup. Bolan made out the lights. The Chevrolet bounced over the rutted road, gaining speed.

5

The hardman who had surrendered inside the machine shop was a rangy, long-jawed man who said his name was Tex Garner. He admitted he had a criminal record but denied he had anything to do with the killing of the six men whose bodies he'd been loading in the van.

The sheriff of Wood County, a lieutenant of the West Virginia State Police and two FBI agents out of the Charleston office joined in the interrogation.

"We'll be checkin' your fingerprints, fella," the police lieutenant warned. "Also that pistol you threw out, to see if any of the slugs from those bodies were fired from it. I figure you're lookin' at a life sentence, and if you know anything about penitentiaries you know the one we got at Moundsville isn't cushy. So you got only one kind of chance—which is to sing like a canary."

Tex Garner flexed his shoulders. His hands were cuffed behind him, and his muscles were beginning to ache. He sat on a bench in the machine shop, surrounded by hostile men, but he didn't look afraid. He just looked furtive, anxious to find a way out of this jam. His eyes returned time and again to Betsy Clendenin, who stood aside calmly smoking a cigarette, still handcuffed, and maybe looking to him like a soul mate, a fellow prisoner. She listened to the talk with unembarrassed curiosity.

Bolan spoke quietly to Shondor Savacheva. "No good work is ever done by committee. There're too many men here."

"I can move in," Shondor offered. "I think they'll all stand aside for the Justice Department."

"Let the state cop have a go at it," Bolan replied. "He's off to a good start."

The lieutenant glared at Garner. "Well? Yes or no?"

Garner shook his head. "I don't know much."

"Tell us what you do know."

"I worked for the fella that got away. Which figured. He *would* get away. Son of a bitch..."

"Major Isaac Stamford," Shondor prompted. "What's he up to, Garner?"

The guy shook his head. "I don't know, man. They were refitting these trucks here. He hired me just tonight, said I could help him clean up a mess. I came here with him and, well, you know. Corpses."

"You weren't surprised," Shondor said. "We heard every word you said, and you knew what was here. But never mind that. Where were the trucks going?"

"Don't know, man."

Shondor turned to the lieutenant of the state police. "How do you execute murderers in West Virginia?"

"We don't," the lieutenant replied. "But they never get out. I mean, never. They die in the pen. Put it another way. We have capital punishment. But it's slow. It takes forty years sometimes. A little bit every day."

"Where did the trucks go, Garner?" Shondor demanded.

Garner looked up at the lieutenant. "What deal?"

The lieutenant shrugged. "Better than you're gonna get the other way."

Garner looked around, seeking the faces of the men who confronted him as if he hoped to see some sign of sympathy. The muscles in his neck tensed.

"They fitted a bunch of trucks with big lead tanks."

"How many trucks?" Bolan asked.

"'Bout ten."

"Why? What for?"

"I don't know for sure, but I gotta figure it's got something to do with the way people been stealing radioactive stuff. Those trucks are all big tankers, and they've been putting lead liners inside. They were driven away from here just after dark. All of 'em."

"To *where*, dammit?"

"Honest to God, I don't know! But it was the Japanese and that other foreigner who killed the guys who did the work. I swear to God I didn't shoot any of those men! You ain't gonna find any slugs from my gun in those bodies. You *ain't*. I saw it, though. The man . . . you call him Major Stamford. Okay. We went off and had some hamburgers. Stamford, he wanted to be sure nobody heard the shooting and no cops would be around here when we came back. So we ate hamburgers down the road and then came back to get the bodies out of here. And we were gonna drive the cars away. The man didn't want it known, for a day or two anyway, that those guys were dead. After a day or two, he said, it wouldn't make any difference."

Bolan stepped forward. "Where'd the trucks go?"

"Honest to God, man, I don't know."

The warrior reached into the holster and withdrew the Desert Eagle. "You saw what this did to your buddies," he said leveling the muzzle toward Garner's belly.

The man licked his lips. "Why do you think I give up?" he whispered hoarsely. "I ain't no coward. I'd shoot it out with most men. Not with you. I don't know who the hell you are, but—'' He shook his head.

One of the FBI agents grabbed Bolan's arm. "We'll never get a conviction if you make him talk this way," he muttered in Bolan's ear.

Bolan glowered at him.

Shondor grabbed the agent by the arm and wrestled him away. "Keep your mouth shut and keep out of the way," he growled.

"Okay," Bolan said to Garner. "You're no coward. So where were the trucks going?"

"I don't know!" Garner protested, staring at the muzzle of the big automatic. "Honest to God, man! I don't know."

"Never heard a name? Where were you going when you left here?"

"Where the man said. That's all I know. Hey! I did hear a name...Buckley. He said something to Homma about going to Buckley. Yeah. We were going to Buckley. Wherever that is."

"IT'S NOT THE NAME of a town," Bolan said to the lieutenant of the West Virginia State Police as they scanned a map, looking for a place called Buckley. "It's got to be the name of a mine. I figure they're hiding the radioactive material in a mine, probably abandoned. Is there a mine called Buckley? A mine operator named Buckley?"

"We can find out at nine in the morning," the lieutenant replied. "When the Bureau opens."

"Nine in the morning may be too late," said Bolan. "Get on the horn and get somebody out of bed. We need to know right now!"

WHEN BOLAN and the others arrived at the home of Brad Buckley—a square frame house on the lower slope of a mountainside—they found the lights on and the family awake at 4:00 a.m.

An old car seat served as a couch on the front porch, and Buckley dropped down on it and closed his hands over his face.

"I should have known," he said. "I should have figured. You deal with that kind of men, you—" He stopped and shook his head. "But I didn't know whether to call the sheriff or not. And right now, with all of you here—that may make them kill her. Just seeing your cars here."

His daughter had been kidnapped.

"He called around five o'clock last night and said he had June. Said just keep my mouth shut and don't talk to anybody, then she'd be let loose and it'd be okay."

"Who called?" Bolan asked.

"A Japanese guy."

"Isoroku Akada," Shondor said.

Buckley shook his head. "Never got his name exactly, but he's Japanese for sure."

"He's using your mine."

Again Buckley shook his head. "What's a man gonna do? Business goes bust and I've a family to support. I don't know what they're doing. I guessed it was something illegal."

Bolan looked at the sky. A faint gray had begun to show against the black. Sunrise was less than an hour away.

"We don't have much time," he said. "If they're moving today, they'll likely move soon. If they haven't already."

"You're going after them? What about my kid?"

"What about ten thousand other kids?"

"Ten . . . thousand? What—"

"You've got to take us to the mine. Or tell us where to find it," Bolan told him.

Brad Buckley glanced at the small circle of grim-faced men. They weren't crazy, and they were heavily armed. He knew an Uzi when he saw one, and he recognized the big man in front of him as a man determined and ready to do what he had to do.

"Leave a couple men to guard my family?" Buckley asked.

Captain Dan Follet of the West Virginia State Police nodded. "Couple of Boone County deputies," he said.

Buckley nodded unhappily and went inside the house. A moment later they heard the man's wife cry out in fear, but he reappeared, carrying a hunting rifle in one hand and a .38 revolver in a holster in the other.

BOLAN HAD CHANGED into a combat blacksuit. Various implements of war hung from his military webbing, including a 9 mm Uzi machine pistol, extra ammo, four grenades, a knife and a coil of rope. The big .44 Desert Eagle was a comfortable and familiar weight on the warrior's right thigh.

"Who the hell is he?" one of the FBI men whispered to Shondor.

"Colonel Pollock is a specialist," the Justice agent replied. "He fights terrorists."

The attack force consisted of Bolan and Shondor, several state and federal agents and officers—as well as Brad Buckley who couldn't be discouraged from joining the group.

"Is this the only road up to the mine?" Bolan asked.

Buckley nodded. "My road. Private."

"We've got to block it," the warrior stated. "Got an ax? Let's get a couple of trees down across it."

"I got an ax in my truck," Buckley offered.

Brad Buckley refused to stay and cut trees while Bolan and the others advanced along the road. Two of the state troopers had to remain behind to carry out the task, then join the others when they were finished.

The Executioner led the way, with Buckley walking beside him, telling him about the slag heaps and how they would make good firing positions.

"Hold it." The warrior had heard the sound of a laboring engine. He turned and ran back toward the two state troopers.

The trees were still heavily laden with leaves. Though they were turning yellow, the leaves hadn't fallen, and the woods still provided cover. Shondor followed Bolan, and just before they reached the place where the two state troopers had now taken a station in the middle of the road, he raced across to be on the opposite side.

"Hey!" Bolan called at the two policemen. "Take cover. These guys aren't going to stop."

The two frowned skeptically but walked into the woods on the east side of the road.

A big tanker came into view, an old veteran of a truck, powerfully and slowly grinding its way up the rough and rutted mountain road, moving ponderously at no more than the speed a man could walk.

Bolan waited for the tanker to reach the point where he stood on a little bank just above the road. As it passed him, he jumped onto the running board and stuck the muzzle of the Desert Eagle through the window and into the driver's face.

The driver stopped the truck. The man riding with him leaned forward to retrieve an Uzi that lay on the floor in front of him, but before he could reach it he felt a cold circle of steel pressing into the side of his neck. Shondor encouraged the man to sit back slowly.

"Okay," Bolan said to the state troopers. "Take these guys into the woods and handcuff them to a tree. Don't bother to chop down any more trees. This truck barricades the road."

Shondor raised the hood of the tractor and used the ax on the engine. In a minute he had totally disabled it.

Bolan trotted up the mountainside again, leaving two state troopers behind to take care of any more vehicles that came up the blocked road. In a couple of minutes he reached the slag heaps. Buckley had led the group up the slope of one of the heaps, and they lay behind the crest, hidden from the mine entrance, which was less than fifty yards away.

Captain Follet had put aside the hat that would have instantly identified him to anyone who saw him, and lay nearest the top, occasionally raising his head to have a look. He spoke into his hand radio, giving orders to every state police unit within fifty miles to stop any tank truck they saw. "Armed and dangerous," he was saying as Bolan crawled up beside him.

Keeping his chin close to the slag, the warrior examined the mine clearing.

Two big tankers were in the rough area between the mouth of the mine and the slag. One was backed up to the mine, as close as possible, and the other was parked to the side, engine running. A little mine cart sat on a pair of narrow-gauge tracks, and a pump labored to empty something from a small tank on the cart into the huge tank on the truck.

What was going on was plain enough—what was strange was that the five men working the pump and controlling the hose were shackled and almost naked. They stumbled barefoot over rough slag, jerking awkwardly against their chains. They worked under the watchful eyes of half a dozen armed guards.

Bolan spoke to Follet. "We've got a tanker disabled on the road, which blocks it. Two of your men are watching for more trucks coming up."

The captain nodded. His attention was focused on the scene below—the chained men laboring to pump sludge from the little mine carts into the tanker truck.

"I know who those fellows are," he said. "Look at 'em. See the cuffs on their wrists, extra shackles on their legs? Escapees. We had a plague of escapes a short time back—somebody helping crooks escape from custody, most of them on their way to the pen. Looks like somebody wanted some slave labor."

"They're killing them," Bolan replied. "Anyone working in contact with that stuff is going to die. That's why the gunmen are keeping their distance."

As the warrior watched, one of the men staggered away from the tanker, dropped to his knees and began to vomit.

"Radiation sickness," Bolan muttered.

Follet reached behind him and took a pair of binoculars from a state trooper. He peered through them at the man.

"Farrell," the captain said quietly, "unless I'm mistaken. He escaped from a station wagon carrying him and some others to the pen. He was going to do life for murder. Nice fellow. Killed a man who had the guts to run for the presidency of a Teamsters Union local against the man chosen by the leadership. I'm pretty damn sure that's who he is."

A woman in chains stumbled out of the mine entrance, and lurched her way toward the fallen man.

One of the gunmen shouted, and the woman stopped. The gunner raised a rifle to his shoulder, took aim and fired one shot. The doomed man rolled over, bloody and dead. Gesturing with the barrel of the rifle, the guard ordered the woman back into the mine. She hobbled away, weeping.

"Priorities," Bolan muttered to the captain. "First, what they're doing has got to be stopped. Saving the child has to be second. It can't be helped."

Follet glanced over his shoulder at the anxious father of the child Bolan was talking about. He nodded.

"The child isn't here," the warrior continued. "Neither is the Shark. At least one of those gunmen knows where he is. There's no telephone line out of here, so I'd guess somebody down there is carrying a radio. You see our problem? We can't let the man with the radio transmit a warning to the Shark, but we can't just kill him. We need him alive, so we can find out from him where the boss is."

"So what do we do?"

"First thing, send some men back to the truck blocking the road. Have them and your other men go back down the hill a lot farther, so if they're involved in a shootout with the next truck they stop, these guys won't hear it."

"Okay."

"I'll go around and come up on the mine entrance from the wooded side. Maybe I can get close enough to grab the radioman."

Follet stared at Bolan for a long moment. "Don't get too close to that stuff they're loading."

"You got it." The warrior slid back from the crest of the slag, stood and trotted away.

Shondor followed him. "It needs two men," he said.

Brad Buckley ran after them. "Hey! It's my kid that's— you've gotta tell me what's going on."

Bolan explained quickly, then added, "What you've got to do is stay here and out of sight."

"Me? Me, who's walked over every square foot of this hill a thousand times? While you go stalking around? Hell, man, you'll fall in a hole. I'm comin' with you."

Bolan considered the situation for a moment, facing the unshaven, haunted-eyed man—a big, hard-muscled guy in boots, worn blue jeans and a red-and-black wool jacket. He looked at the man's hunting rifle—well-worn but obviously prized and lovingly cared for. It must have been passed down in the Buckley family—an old Winchester bolt-action, chambered for .30-06 rounds. The stock was checkered, and the checkering had been kept clean of mud and grease. The wood had been kept polished, and the barrel and action gleamed.

It would have been useless to tell Brad Buckley that he had to stay back. Shondor agreed. "I'll stay here with the locals. Follet may be a little trigger-happy, so it's maybe a good idea for one of us to stay with him."

Bolan nodded at Buckley, and the man strode off, taking the lead.

The Executioner had intended to back off down the hill, cross the road and come up on the mine entrance from his right. Buckley circled the end of the slag heaps to their left, entered the brush and slipped downhill no more than twenty yards, then began to climb the wooded hill to the left of the mine. It was a faster way to move.

Buckley had been right in warning that there were obscure pits in the woods, vents from the mine shaft, once sheathed with wood, now collapsed and hidden by brush. In minutes they were above the mine, in heavy underbrush.

From his new position Bolan could see the slave laborers as Follet had seen them through his binoculars—men with sick, hollow faces, stumbling through the paces of work they knew was killing them. He couldn't focus on them for long. He had to look for the radio, if there was one.

The guards sat on the slope above the entrance to the mine and supervised the work from a distance. They were Americans, from the look of them—hardmen, the kind you could hire to do any dirty work, the kind of men who could sit and coldly watch men just like themselves dying of radiation poisoning and never give it a thought. They were the kind he had fought for years. They were armed in all manner of weapons—pistols, submachine guns and rifles.

But a radio? Maybe he'd guessed wrong. Maybe they didn't communicate with Akada. Maybe one of them had all the authority he needed. Or maybe Akada was somewhere around. Could they be that lucky? Lucky enough to catch the Japanese? No, not likely. There *had* to be a way of communicating.

Buckley touched his shoulder. "Look," he whispered.

The mine owner had noticed that one of the men was different—clean-shaven, thinner, dressed, unlike the others, in khaki pants and a dark blue nylon jacket. Bolan focused on him. Oh, yeah . . . he'd seen him before. In the Blennerhasset Truck Repairs shop. Major Isaac Stamford. He wore a Cincinnati Reds baseball cap that covered his bald head, but he was the man who'd escaped last night. He wore a .45 Colt on his right hip in an Army-style holster. Sure. The cashiered Marine officer, accustomed to command and in command the way he'd been last night.

And sure enough, it was hung on his left hip—a little leather holster and a Handie-Talkie radio.

"How we gonna do it?" Buckley whispered.

"*I'm* gonna do it," Bolan answered. "Don't fire a shot. If you do, the police on the slag pile will open fire. You watch from up here. Unless you see me in big trouble, just watch."

"You know what you're doin', don't you?"

"I've had a little experience with this kind of thing," he commented dryly.

It was time to use that experience again. No matter how often Bolan became embroiled in a firefight, it was never easy. He checked the Desert Eagle and the Uzi, then slipped off into the brush to the right of the mine.

The guards kept their distance from the deadly sludge. They kept fifty yards and more back from the tanker and the mine carts. There were eight of them spread out on the hillside above the mine. Another pair stood where the road entered the clearing, holding guns leveled on the mine entrance.

Stamford, who had stalked back and forth along the slope for a few minutes, now sat down in the grass, a little apart from the others, and began to unwrap a sandwich. The air of command. An officer kept himself a little apart from his men.

But only a little apart. There was no way to take him without the others seeing.

Bolan worked his way around the wooded hillside until he was above Stamford and behind him. From there he could see the sludge going into the tanker. The stream from the pump was thick and oily, an evil, lethal muck capable of carrying death to a hundred times the number of people who had died on Majorca.

Stamford barked something at two of the gunmen, and they advanced down the slope, guns raised, yelling at the slaves.

"C'mon! C'mon! We ain't got all day. Move it, unless you want to end up like your buddy there."

Major Stamford popped the tab on a can of Coke, and Bolan moved silently closer.

Two of the chained men climbed onto the tanker, closed the hatch and secured it. Then they hosed down the vehicle until no trace of the black oily sludge remained. Only then did the driver cautiously climb into the cab.

The movement of the truck and bringing the second one into place to receive its load distracted the men on the slope and made it possible for Bolan to move in closer still.

Now he was a scant ten yards behind Stamford.

Bolan slung the Uzi over his shoulder and drew the Desert Eagle. Nothing but a thin cover of briars with yellow leaves and red berries remained between him and Stamford. The warrior covered the ten yards in seconds. Three or four gunmen saw him move, but none was quick enough to stop him before he had reached Major Stamford and pressed the muzzle of the Desert Eagle to the back of his neck.

"On your feet," Bolan growled.

The major held his hands to his sides as he slowly rose from the ground. Bolan lifted the Colt .45 from its holster and the little radio from its case.

The hardmen saw what had happened and they formed a semicircle around Bolan and the major, threatening with enough firepower to tear both of them to shreds. The Executioner's left arm was clamped around his captive's throat, and his right hand pressed the muzzle of the .44 Magnum to the man's skull.

"Talk to them," Bolan grunted.

"Back away," Stamford ordered curtly. "I think I know who this guy is, and he's not alone. Back off! Now!"

Like sullen snarling dogs, the hardmen backed slowly away—except one man, who stepped forward and confronted Bolan and the major with an Uzi.

"Haley!" the major yelled. "You have your orders!"

Haley grinned and shook his head. He was a fat bearded man, wearing a blue-gray checkered wool shirt and a nylon cap with the John Deere logo on the front.

"Haley..."

"I've got my orders all right," Haley sneered, "from Mr. Akada. Now, bogeyman, whoever you are in the black suit, we're gonna find out somethin'. I'm bettin' a bunch of parabellum slugs will come right through Stamford and get you, same burst.''

"Haley!"

"My orders are to get rid of you, Stamford, sooner or later. I'd figured on later—not too much later, though. Before you got a chance to kill *me*, that's all. But now's as good a time as any.''

The hardmen stood in their ragged semicircle, watching with dumb curiosity. None of them made so much as a gesture toward interfering.

The slaves had stopped working and stood staring at the confrontation on the slope above them.

Haley began a deep, rumbling chuckle as he slowly raised the muzzle of the Uzi.

Bolan had slipped the muzzle of the Desert Eagle away from the major's neck, and the barrel now lay on Stamford's shoulder.

Haley was right that the 9 mm slugs from the Uzi would blast right through Stamford. Bolan could only hope that he'd have a chance to aim the .44 and that a slug would knock Haley off his feet in the first half second of his burst.

Haley laughed aloud, the odd sound echoing off the hill-side.

But his laugh was cut short as his head suddenly exploded. The mocking face was gone. The clean, sharp crack of Buckley's .30-06 also echoed off the hill, followed by the crisp click of the bolt chambering another round.

At this point Captain Follet and the rest of the state and federal troops stood up on the crest of the slag heap, all their weapons aimed at the confused hardmen. Shondor Savacheva loped boldly down the front slope.

The two gunmen in the clearing in front of the mine turned and ran into the woods. Three of the men facing

Bolan dropped their weapons and raised their hands. One raised the muzzle of an M-16, and Shondor dropped him instantly. Then the others surrendered.

The state police and deputies moved down into the clearing. Someone had brought a Geiger counter, and they approached the slaves slowly and cautiously. The escaped prisoners dropped to the ground and sat stupidly on the slag, as if none of them really understood what was happening.

The woman stumbled out of the mine. A trooper took the Geiger counter over to her and ran it over her body. It didn't click. An FBI agent went to her and offered the scantily clad woman his jacket. When the trooper carried the Geiger counter to the group of men, it clicked angrily. No one went near them after that.

Brad Buckley came down from the woods and walked to where Bolan stood over Major Isaac Stamford, who had sunk to the ground.

The Handie-Talkie squawked, and a voice said, "Report. Everything okay?"

Bolan looked hard at Stamford, then he pressed the transmit button and spoke into the little radio. "A little slow, but okay."

"There's no time to waste," the voice replied.

"Right," Bolan said.

The radio went silent, leaving Bolan and Buckley to wonder if the man on the other end of the conversation—undoubtedly the Shark—had suspected he wasn't talking to the major.

Buckley stood above Stamford, glowering. "Where's my daughter?" he asked.

The major looked at him and didn't speak.

"Where's the Shark?" Bolan asked.

Stamford shifted his eyes back and forth between Bolan and Buckley. "You can both go to hell," he snarled.

Buckley pointed the muzzle of his Winchester at Stamford's leg, and before Bolan could stop him he fired a .30-06 slug through Stamford's right knee.

"You'll crawl to the electric chair, you son of a bitch," Buckley growled.

Stamford clutched his shattered, crippled knee and writhed in agony, but he seemed to hear Buckley, and certainly he did see the muzzle of the rifle pointing at his left knee.

"Next is your balls," Buckley threatened. *"Where's my daughter?"*

Major Stamford spoke to Bolan. "Logan," he groaned. "Holiday Inn."

ON THE WAY to Logan, Bolan changed into khaki pants and a red nylon jacket. Shondor had handed him Major Stamford's Cincinnati Reds baseball cap, saying it gave him the appearance of a local. He put aside the Desert Eagle and hung the 93-R Beretta in leather under his left arm. The red jacket also covered his sheathed knife and his coil of rope.

Buckley went with him and Shondor in the car—there was no denying the man—but this time Bolan insisted he stay back.

"He knows you," Bolan said. "If he sees you—"

"I'll be outside with the rifle," Buckley promised. "I might turn out to be the key man here, too."

Bolan and Shondor exchanged glances. They hoped Brad Buckley's pride didn't go before a fall.

"The whole deal," Bolan explained, "is to get your little girl out of there alive. To do that, we don't need heroes. Okay?"

They didn't know for sure if Buckley's daughter was in the motel, but they *did* know that an Oriental man was in room 2B. The desk clerk hadn't seen him with a little girl.

The motel was a two-story cinderblock building, painted white. Rooms on the second floor were reached by rusting steel stairs at each end and by walking along a balcony that ran across the front of the building. Room 2B was the second from the left end on the second floor.

"We've got to get him out of there somehow," Shondor said quietly. "If the child is in that room with him . . . the point is to get him to come out."

Bolan frowned over the walkie-talkie he'd taken from Major Stamford then pressed the transmit button.

"Got a problem," he said into the microphone.

For a moment there was no response. Then, "What problem?"

"Cops."

They waited for a response, but there was none.

"That oughta smoke him out," Shondor muttered.

They stood in the parking lot beside their car. Buckley crouched on the gravel behind the car, out of sight. Bolan and Shondor leaned on the vehicle, trying to look as casual as possible. The Executioner faced the motel building, and it was he who saw the curtains part on the window in 2B. He couldn't see the face behind the glass, but someone was checking the parking lot.

A minute later the door opened and Isoroku Akada stepped out onto the balcony. His left hand gripped a small black suitcase, his right the hand of a little blond girl in blue jeans and a gray sweatshirt.

"We cool it," Bolan said loud enough for Buckley to hear. "He has to come down here to a car."

For a long moment the Japanese stood on the balcony, looking down at the parking lot and especially at the two men—Bolan and Shondor—so casually chatting beside one of the cars. The warrior glanced up once and was careful not to seem to notice him.

"When he gets down here, I'll take him," Bolan whispered to Shondor. "You jump for the child."

"Got it."

But suddenly a shot rang out and Akada staggered back against the brick wall, hit in the left arm or shoulder. Buckley chambered another .30-06 cartridge. Akada shoved the little girl back into the motel room, and before Buckley could fire again he ducked inside and slammed the door.

There was no point in telling Brad Buckley what he'd done. Bolan and Shondor rushed to the motel to be under the balcony and out of Akada's sight. Buckley, now shaking, ran after them.

"You take orders now," Bolan growled to Buckley. "Go into the motel office and tell the clerk to call every room that's occupied. Have him warn the people in those rooms about what's going on. They should stay in their rooms and away from the windows. Then he should call the state police. Go! And don't come back. You stay in the office."

Bolan turned to Shondor. "We could wait him out, I suppose. Buckley did hit him and he's got to do something. What I'm afraid of is, if he decides he's had it, he might kill the child. I mean, he might kill her and then himself. The Shark isn't the kind of man who's going to go out quietly. You stay here and watch him. I'll check the rear of the building."

Shondor nodded, and Bolan went to check out the rear of the building. What he discovered was that every unit in the motel had a rear window. Maybe it had been someone's idea to give guests a view of what was back there, a woodland creek under a rock ledge. Every unit had, in fact, two windows, a small one with frosted glass that obviously was the bathroom window, and a larger window that would be the rear window of the bedroom. The window in 2B was covered by a curtain.

The creek—clear water running over rocks—was only about fifteen feet from the rear wall of the motel. The rock ledge over the creek rose six or eight feet higher than the ground on which the motel stood. Tall trees, their leaves now turning yellow and red, grew behind the ledge and almost to its brink.

Bolan saw what he could do.

He returned to Shondor and outlined his plan.

The warrior circled around the building again and found a point where he could cross the creek and climb to the top of the rock ledge. He backed into the woods far enough to be out of sight from the motel, then worked his way to a point opposite 2B, to where a tall, straight oak grew. It was the tree he'd noticed during his recon. Tossing his rope over the lowest limb, he climbed hand over hand until he reached the limb and could use it to pull himself up. He continued climbing until he was well up into the oak.

Now he had a problem to solve—to choose a limb, knot his rope around it and judge the arc between the tree and the rear window of 2B. He would have only one chance. If he swung across and slammed into the cinderblock wall...

He climbed down to the lowest limb. Standing there, he coiled the rope and tied the coil; then he let the coil swing out across the creek toward the motel. Okay. He could judge it. The coil, if it had completed the arc, which it didn't because it wasn't heavy enough, would have hit the wall under the window. He could see where he would have to grasp the rope.

He had to climb back up to recover the rope. Carrying it back down again, he gripped it tightly and was ready. That window, which had seemed big enough when he looked at it from the ground, seemed like a small target from here. But a child's life was at stake.

Shondor peered around the end of the motel. He'd been checking Bolan's progress every two or three minutes. He spotted Bolan standing on the limb of the oak and threw up his hands. Bolan nodded emphatically. He was ready.

Shondor's role was to grab Akada's attention by pounding on the door of 2B.

When Bolan heard the loud noise, he let himself go. The limb above bent under his weight, and he made an instant adjustment, grabbing higher on the rope as he swung. He drew his body up and thrust his feet out ahead of him. As he reached the bottom of the arc, over the creek, he was swinging at a dizzying speed, but as he swung upward toward the window he slowed a little.

He'd judged right. His feet hit the glass of the window, shattering it and the frame with the tremendous force of his weight moving at what was a fair rate of speed. The force of the swing carried him through the broken window, just as he had hoped. His head grazed the top of the window, and he felt broken glass cutting him on the scalp and arms, but he was inside the room, on his back in a tangle of the heavy fabric that was the drapery.

Akada fired a burst, but he aimed it through the door. He had the child clutched to him with his left hand, and with his right he aimed a silenced Czech automatic.

Bolan tore himself loose from the tangle of drapery and pulled his Beretta.

Akada spun, but he was too slow. His attention had been firmly fixed on the door, and he had required a second to refocus. Holding the screaming child also slowed him. He moved the muzzle of the CZ-52 toward Bolan, but before he could really aim, a silenced 9 mm round from the Beretta tore through his throat.

6

Taiyodi Laqiya sat in a carved wooden armchair that resembled a throne. The resemblance didn't go unnoticed by his collaborators, nor was it meant to. Once more he was dressed in a long white robe, elaborately embroidered in green-and-gold thread. He also wore his trademark sunglasses.

An hour ago he had spoken with his aide Nasira Fouzi. "You see, Nasira? Akada is dead. Vilad is dead. Now the rest of them come to ask for more money. I will not give it until some of their bomb-grade material is delivered. When God wills, they will all be dead. And we will have the material we need."

Fouzi was doubtful, but it made no difference. He would report what he learned from this meeting, which would fatten his Swiss bank account, and by the time the demented leader had overreached himself to the point of assassination, he, Nasira, would no longer live in Sidi.

In the conference room, Laqiya faced Napoleon Malik, Albrecht Kirchner and Hajan Dihanesi. Because his sunglasses obscured his eyes, none of them could tell which one he was looking at—or if he was, perhaps, actually staring out at the palm-shaded garden and the desert beyond.

"It is intolerable," Laqiya declared, "that the righteous peoples of the world are condemned to arming with what the arrogant imperialists call 'poor men's weapons.' Bring me the fissionable material I have paid for! Bring it now, and I will build the weapons to burn the imperialists as they burn the righteous.''

He'd been talking this way for some time. The others had been patient, but now Napoleon Malik spoke up.

''First the imperialists surrender,'' he said firmly in the Arabic that only he, Laqiya and Nasira understood. ''Then we build the weapons to keep them in their place.''

Laqiya sneered. ''You will make them surrender by pouring radioactive materials in their swimming pools?''

''If,'' Malik continued, ''you lay down even the foundations of a nuclear reactor—''

''I don't need a reactor,'' Laqiya interrupted. ''You bring me the bomb-grade material I have already paid you for— and which you hold in your hands—and I will force their surrender within a week.''

Malik shook his head. ''With what we could bring you, you could make ten bombs, maybe fifteen. The imperialists have thousands. The first time one of your bombs bursts over an imperialist city, they would shoot fifty bombs into your country. Archaeologists ten thousand years from now would sift the sands and wonder what once existed here.''

Laqiya's face showed no sign of his reaction.

Malik switched to French and Fouzi moved closer to Laqiya, to translate.

Malik continued to talk. Fouzi couldn't keep up with his rapid, idiomatic French, but he could translate the gist of what the tall, self-confident, dignified Arab said.

''The Americans have kept the river plan quiet. They are afraid, obviously, to terrify their people by allowing them to know we have the power to poison one of their most central rivers. This setback is only that—a setback. We continue to hold a very significant quantity of radioactive materials of various kinds. We can use them as we wish, when we wish.''

Albrecht Kirchner interrupted. "Let us not suppose," he said, "that Isoroku Akada was a fool. Not all failures are the result of any man's inadequacy. The truth is, the Shark ran up against the American devil, Mack Bolan."

"Bolan, Bolan..." Hajan Dihanesi interjected. "Everything bad that happens to the forces of God, wherever in the world, is blamed on this Mack Bolan. I suggest to you that he does not exist."

Kirchner shook his head. "No, my friend. Do not delude yourself. Bolan is very real, and there is much reason to believe that the Shark was murdered by him."

Fouzi's translation was slow, but it was fast enough for Laqiya to interrupt Kirchner's last words and say to Malik in Arabic, "Then this Bolan person must be eliminated."

Malik nodded at the white-robed figure behind the over-sized sunglasses. "Some very good men have thought so over the years. Bolan lives, and they are dead."

"I fear no one!"

"We would have more respect for you if you did," Malik replied.

Kirchner had closed his eyes and waited out Laqiya's interruption with mock patience. "For too long," he said, "this Bolan has been—"

"Are you agreeing with the Divine Leader?" Malik asked in French, the language that excelled almost any other in letting him put sarcastic emphasis on the phrase "Divine Leader."

Fouzi didn't translate the sarcasm.

Kirchner appreciated the irony and smiled. "If we could eliminate Bolan, it would be almost as valuable an achievement as the rest of it," he said. "I suggest we forget small demonstrations of the power we have acquired and move to the war. I suggest that we make the elimination of Bolan a concurrent project. Surely we have the resources to undertake both these responsibilities at the same time."

Malik nodded. "Let us, Brother Kirchner, be specific..."

NASIRA FOUZI had recorded the meeting on videotape. The Divine Leader stared thoughtfully at a few minutes of it, then turned his interest away. He couldn't understand most of the languages used, so he had to rely on his aide's translations; and reliance on any man for anything demanded of him a concession he fervently disliked making.

The general then left the conference center for his tent city five miles away, and Fouzi was left in the control room of the taping center, scanning the monitors that displayed what the television cameras saw in the suites of every man who had attended the meeting.

Most of it was unworthy of his attention—middle-aged men in their bathrooms attending to the calls of nature, drinking great quantities of alcohol, which the Divine Leader hadn't provided over dinner, accepting the attentions of the young women the leader had provided in the hope that the tapes of what happened in the beds would afford him some influence over these men. All of it would be taped, and almost all of what they would view in the morning would be indescribably dull.

But maybe not what happened in Malik's room. Fouzi sat before the monitor showing Napoleon Malik lying on his bed.

He'd brought the woman, the one he called Jasmin Malik and offered to the world as his wife. The story of her was that she had been caught selling hashish in Pakistan, had been flogged in the forecourt of a mosque, then imprisoned in a dungeon, from which Malik had bought her. What

Nasira saw on the television monitor now confirmed the story. Jasmin Malik was naked, and when she turned her back to the camera he could see the thick and shiny scars of a cruel whipping that had slashed her skin from her shoulders to her upper legs.

They talked.

"A commitment to kill Bolan," she said. "Quite a goal."

"I suspect he was among the gunmen shooting at us in Paris. This man often pops up in the least likely places. You know what they call him? The Executioner.

"In the meeting," Malik continued, "Kirchner agreed to accept the assignment to rid the world of this Executioner."

Jasmin Malik shrugged. Nasira couldn't help admiring her. She was tall, stately in her bearing, exquisitely formed, her face thin and noble, her hands slender and expressive, and on the whole an obviously shrewd, capable woman. But for the ugly scars on her back and what they represented, she could have been an aristocrat of Islam.

"Kirchner," she sneered. "A fat potato-eating German."

"So," Malik said, "we let this German distract Bolan while we fix our attention on the important work. Frankly I'm happy to send this lumpy man away on an errand, while Dihanesi and I manage the vital project."

"Where do we strike, Napoleon?"

Malik grinned. She rarely called him Napoleon, and when she did it was a satirical comment, suggesting that he avoid delusions of grandeur. "Jasmin, why do things in a small way? We will decide. But why not think in terms of Paris, Rome, London, New York?"

"Put the stuff in the water supply?" she asked.

"Some cities depend on reservoirs," Malik replied. "They don't defend the circumferences of those reservoirs. They can't, except by keeping large armies on duty all around them.''

Jasmine laughed. "The world will shudder!" Her face quickly darkened. "And then, Napoleon, you will keep your promise to me."

Malik nodded. "When we rule," he promised, "we will summon before our court the mullahs who hurt you. Then...then, my darling, you will enjoy the pleasure of castrating them with a dull knife!"

She smiled dreamily. "I have five of them in mind. They still live, Napoleon. You have promised them to me."

"I keep my promises."

DAVID SYRKIN sat at a table in a sidewalk café in Palermo. His curly dark hair, his olive complexion, his casual clothes—including a khaki windbreaker and a wool cap— suggested a native Sicilian, though no real Sicilian failed to notice the presence of a stranger on the street. Syrkin's leg, which had been injured in the shootout in Montparnasse, had nearly healed. He still favored that leg and walked with a minor limp, but he was essentially fit.

The Sicilians who watched and judged him from a distance guessed that he carried a weapon under that jacket. He could be in Palermo carrying a gun for many reasons, and as long as his business had nothing to do with the special conditions there—with the operations of the Friends of the Friends—they weren't interested in him.

Syrkin, left to his own desires and without obligation to try to help solve the problems of the world, would have lived his life like this: his face turned to the Mediterranean, his favorite of all seas, sipping a pleasant Mediterranean wine, contemplating a heaping platter of the pasta with seafood that would soon satisfy his appetite.

Unhappily, quiet contemplation of a blue sea, wine and good food was not his fate. He was an agent of Mossad, and his obsession was the salvation of his country—lately, the salvation of the world, if that were not egomania.

So where was the damned Sidian?

Finally the man came, as conspicuous as an elephant in his black, double-breasted suit, with a gray hat that didn't fit him. David wondered what he wore at home and why he hadn't worn it here. In a toga he wouldn't have been as obvious as he was in that suit and hat.

"I brought the stuff," he said in French as he sat down.

Nasira Fouzi had run his final mission, come to collect enough money to support him for the rest of his life...somewhere.

"Videotapes?" Syrkin asked.

"Exactly as promised."

FORTY MINUTES LATER a tall, strikingly handsome woman left the Grande Albergo delle Palme, a hotel in the center of the city. She carried a black leather attaché case. At the door she asked for a taxi and, within the hearing of the doorman, asked to be driven to the airport. A few minutes after the driver pulled away from the hotel she told him she had changed her mind and wanted to be taken to the Grand Hotel Villa Igiea.

She was annoyed. The black briefcase was packed with Swiss francs. Fouzi had already met the Israeli and taken payment for the tapes, but Malik hadn't found the Israeli.

"They will find Fouzi," she told him, "when the maid comes in to turn down his bed. Not before, I should think. And I have no reason to suppose they will identify me with his death. Even so, we should be away from here before they find him. There is no point in trying to hunt for the Mossad agent. We'll never find him now."

Malik stared at the bundles of notes in the attaché case. "Not all is lost," he said. "That looks like a tidy sum."

"We should drive to Messina and take the ferry," Jasmin suggested. "And I think we should go now."

Napoleon Malik's eyes narrowed. He didn't like taking orders, not even strong suggestions, from a woman. It wasn't a woman's place, even, to give advice. And this woman... It didn't help that she was right. It didn't help that she was the most coldly effective person he knew. He kept his peace for the moment. It seemed he kept it more and more often as time passed.

"REGARDEZ!"

Paul Lemaire pointed at the scars on Jasmin Malik's back.

The interpreter droned on, translating Arabic into English for Mack Bolan, as another interpreter had translated into French for Lemaire.

"You see! They'll kill you if they can!"

"I'd take that seriously if I were you, Bolan," Syrkin warned.

"Kirchner," Lemaire said, "is assigned to murder Bolan. He's a very dangerous man. Clever and ruthless."

"Within half an hour after Fouzi sold these tapes to me, he was murdered in his hotel room," Syrkin informed them. "The Italian police don't have a suspect. *I* do. The woman you see on the tape, Jasmin Malik, was in that hotel that morning. Or if not Jasmin Malik, then a strikingly beautiful Pakistani woman. The Italian police don't want to think a woman murdered Fouzi. *I* think she did."

"New York, Los Angeles, London, Moscow." Bolan shook his head. "It was partly luck that we stopped them from dumping tons of radioactive sludge into the Ohio River. But dump it into a municipal water supply and the city would have to be evacuated. Can you imagine trying to evacuate a city the size of New York? It would be a nightmare.''

Paul Lemaire sighed loudly. He rose from the table, stepped to the window and looked down on the bustling streets of Lisbon, where they had agreed to meet as an accommodation to Syrkin.

''What city?'' Bolan asked. ''What reservoir? They're fed by streams. They could dump the stuff into any stream that feeds a reservoir.''

''Very few cities are supplied by only one reservoir,'' Syrkin said, ''but introducing deadly radioactivity into any one reservoir will poison a whole water-supply system.''

''The key,'' Bolan suggested, ''is to stop them before they get close. In West Virginia they were only hours from dumping their sludge into a river that feeds the Ohio River. Just hours, and we were lucky we got to them in time. Every Intelligence agency, Mossad, GIGN, MI-6, the CIA…all of them have to turn every resource to this threat. *Every resource!*''

''BOLAN MUST NOT be told,'' the President said. He rose from behind his desk in the Oval Office and walked to one of the glass doors, from which he had a view of the Washington Monument, all but obscured now by a pelting autumn rain. He turned away from the door and faced Hal Brognola. ''Do you agree?''

Brognola nodded. ''I think you're right.''

The President sighed.

Brognola frowned over the paper the President had handed him a couple of minutes earlier. It was a letter from the United Righteous.

To the President of the United States

Not a single demand made in our proclamation, issued after our small demonstration on the island of Majorca of the new power possessed by the soldiers of the oppressed peoples, has been met. You may, perhaps, believe that because your Gestapo murderers interfered with our next demonstration in Middle America that you have defeated us. Do not be deceived. We are neither defeated nor discouraged.

Our next action will not be a small demonstration of the righteous anger of the oppressed. We will visit retribution on the slave drivers of the world.

To postpone this retribution while you and your fellow slave drivers discuss your surrender, you may meet one more demand. It must be met immediately, without delay, without tricks.

The bandit-murderer Bolan must be destroyed! He must be destroyed and his body displayed, so we can be sure he is dead. We declare war on him! Your alliance with him will cost you dear! The body of the bandit-murderer must be placed on display in a public place in a dwelling place of righteous people, that the oppressed may see and examine.

You have five days in which to comply!

The United Righteous

"Even if Bolan was inclined to sacrifice himself to stave off their next attack, I wouldn't accept the idea," the President said.

"If we gave them Bolan, whose life would they want next, Mr. President?" Brognola asked. "Yours?"

The President shrugged, then he smiled. "Maybe yours, Hal. It doesn't make any difference. We don't make this kind of deal."

Brognola handed the paper back to the President. "It's odd that they haven't released any of their proclamations and demands to the news media. It makes me wonder about something."

"What?"

"Will they come along one of these days and amend their whole set of demands? Will they suddenly tell us that what they want is a very large sum of money? You never know for sure, when you're dealing with this kind of people, whether you're dealing with fanatics or just plain criminals."

"Do they want to 'free the oppressed,' or just get rich?" The President nodded. "You have to wonder."

"The ones we've identified do quite well for themselves," Brognola went on. "Malik, Kirchner and, before he died, Akada. The champions of the 'oppressed' are not themselves *of* the oppressed."

"At least we have to warn Bolan."

"He's already been warned," Brognola replied. "He's in Lisbon right now, viewing a videotape secured by Mossad."

"Be sure he knows that the man who made that tape is already dead."

BOLAN WAS ACTUALLY aboard a 747 on its way to Kennedy International Airport, New York. He'd had a call from Shondor Savacheva, who would meet him at Kennedy. From there they would fly on to California in a government plane.

"Hey, man," Shondor had told him on the phone. "Something may be coming down. They've found a high level of radioactivity in Mono Lake, and that's part of the Los Angeles water supply. It's hundreds of miles from L.A., but the streams that feed that lake also feed the Los Angeles Aqueduct. I mean, they steer water out of some of those streams and into the aqueduct. It may be nothing but, man, if it is..."

The conversation was revived when they were on board the government airplane. "It may be something important," Bolan said. "Whichever, we're not doing anything else right now."

"It involves a new element," Shondor told him. "Everything until now has been kept secret. This isn't. It was reported in the *Los Angeles Times* on Friday. Everybody's looking at Mono Lake. If somebody wanted to create panic—"

"How'd they find out about this radioactivity? Somebody send a warning?"

"No. Routine check."

"Can they close the aqueduct?"

Shondor nodded. "They say they don't have to. Not yet. They're monitoring the water and assuring Los Angeles that the water is absolutely safe and that they can cut it off the minute they find anything bad."

"Doesn't sound like the United Righteous," Bolan said.

"No. We may be off on a wild-goose chase. Anyway, you hungry? Thirsty?"

"Sleepy," Bolan replied. "I sat beside a nonstop talker all the way from Lisbon to New York. Think I'll catch some shut-eye."

They landed at the airport at Bishop, California, a little before 1:00 a.m., were met by an FBI agent from the San Francisco office and were driven to a Best Western Motel. Bolan's catnap had refreshed him, and the three men—Bolan, Shondor and the agent, whose name was Frank Colicci, sat down in the bar for a late drink. Shondor had introduced Bolan as Colonel Pollock.

"I'm afraid you've come out here on a wild-goose chase, gentlemen," Colicci began. "It turns out that the scientists have known for years that Lake Mono is radioactive."

"How? Why?" Shondor asked.

"Nobody knows for sure. Illegal dumping, likely. There's a rumor that the Navy once set off a bomb underwater for a test, but the Navy denies it, and the kinds of radioactive material they're finding look more like nuclear-plant waste than anything from an underwater shot."

"Maybe they're trying to play the thing down to make Los Angeles feel safer," Bolan suggested.

"Could be," said Colicci.

"Is the lake more radioactive today than it was two weeks ago?" Bolan asked.

"Oh, yeah. That's why everybody's so excited."

"Did the new radioactivity come in from the feeder streams?" Bolan asked.

Colicci shook his head. "They don't think so. On the other hand, we're talking about mountain streams, clear water running fast. Something dumped into the headwaters of one of those streams could run into the lake in an hour, leaving the streambed pretty much clean. You'd have to go upstream and find pools to find traces. Anyway, they aren't finding any radioactivity in the water diverted into the L.A. water system."

Bolan exchanged glances with Shondor. "Unless it's a test."

"Like I said, I'm afraid you've been called out here for nothing. In the morning I'll take you up to the EPA station on the lake and introduce you to the scientists."

In the morning Bolan was treated to inspiring views of some of the world's most spectacular scenery. Mono Lake edged Yosemite National Park, and high forested mountains rose on both sides of the highway Colicci drove on.

But their visit to the brackish and now faintly radioactive lake was, as Colicci had warned, a waste of time. The scientists were cooperative, but it appeared not only that the radioactivity in the water was the result of illegal industrial dumping but that it was the result of *old* dumping. Unusually heavy rains had caused a heavy flow of runoff into the lake, stirring up radioactive materials that had long lain on the bottom.

Or so the scientists guessed. They really didn't know.

The Lear remained ready for takeoff on the field at Bishop, so Bolan and Shondor decided to return to the East Coast. Having expected to stay another day, they hadn't checked out of the motel and had left their clothes and some weapons there. They picked up their things from their rooms while Colicci checked them out.

Bolan traveled light. He wore khakis, with a khaki nylon jacket—in keeping with his persona as a retired colonel— and carried a duffel bag. He had a suit carefully folded in the nylon bag, in the event he needed to dress up. More important, the Desert Eagle was in the bag. The Beretta 93-R was snug in leather inside his khaki jacket.

Colicci had been quick in the motel office and was waiting beside the unmarked government Buick when Bolan and Shondor came down from their room.

Colicci shouted a warning at the exact instant Bolan heard the metallic thump of a grenade on the blacktop. He spun and kicked it as hard as he could. Propelled by Bolan's kick, the grenade skidded under a gray Toyota, where it went off with a roar, lifting the car off its wheels. Except for a few pellets that shot across the pavement—one hitting Shondor on the ankle and giving him a bloody wound—the steel pellets hurled by the explosion punctured the gas tank and the tires, and the Toyota settled flat onto the blacktop and burst into flame.

Bolan grabbed Shondor by the arm and helped him limp behind a Chevrolet. He expected another grenade at any moment.

Colicci had drawn his government-issue Beretta and was firing one shot after another toward the room from which the grenade had been thrown.

In response, a burst of automatic fire ripped across the parking lot, wide of Bolan and Shondor.

Bolan hadn't yet identified which room the gunman had fired from, and he couldn't be sure that the gunman had lobbed the grenade. Several windows were open, and as he peered up, searching for the gunner, a woman in a pink jogging suit appeared at a window.

"Get back!" Colicci yelled. "Get down!"

For a long moment the woman stood there as if numb, staring at the burning car and the armed men in the parking lot. Finally a man appeared behind her and pulled her back.

Shondor sat on the ground behind the Chevrolet, binding his ankle with a sleeve he'd ripped from his nylon jacket.

Bolan, who was crouched behind the next car, had extended the little front handgrip on his Beretta. With his left thumb hooked through the extended trigger guard and his fingers tight around that forward handgrip, he could steady his aim so well that he achieved almost the accuracy he would have with a rifle.

"Ready," Shondor called. He'd bound up his leg and had pulled his Beretta—not a 93-R, like Bolan's, but the 92 the government had widely adopted. "Let's get the son of a bitch."

"Hang tight," Bolan replied. "Be ready for another grenade."

Almost on cue a second metallic orb flew from a window and landed on the parking lot, rolling toward the cars. The fuse made no smoke, but heat spurted visibly from the hand bomb as it rolled toward the Chevrolet.

Shondor scrambled onto the back of the Chevrolet, and Bolan jumped onto the rear of the Pontiac.

The grenade rolled under the Chevrolet and exploded, its explosion and storm of steel pellets expended on the undercarriage of the vehicle. The Chevy rocked on its suspension, then settled on its wheels, the tires shredded by hurtling pellets.

A torrent of slugs tore through the Chevrolet, whipping its glass into a storm of flying shards.

Bolan realized by now that the grenades and gunfire did come from one window. He set the 93-R to 3-round burst, took aim on the window and fired. The subsonic rounds left the pistol with a subdued burp. The curtains whipped back, and he thought he saw a man stagger away from the window. He couldn't be sure.

Colicci trotted down the line of parked cars. "I've radioed for help," he called, crouching to the ground behind a green Mercedes, two cars away from Bolan's position. "All we need to do is sit tight until the local police surround the place."

"If they figure they're trapped," Shondor told him, "they'll do something tough to make an escape."

Bolan steadied his Beretta and fired a single shot to remind them he was out there.

A grenade suddenly flew from the window, and Bolan, Shondor and Colicci threw themselves flat against the ground.

Whoever had tossed the previous grenades had learned from his mistakes. This time he'd thrown the grenade harder, and the lethal egg hit a car, rolled over the top of the Mercedes that sheltered Colicci, and dropped at his feet.

NO COST! NO OBLIGATION TO PURCHASE!

PLAY "LUCKY 7" AND GET AS MANY AS FIVE FREE GIFTS...

HOW TO PLAY

1. Get a coin and scratch off the silver area at the right. This makes you eligible to receive as many as four free books and a surprise mystery gift, depending on what is revealed beneath the scratch-off area.

2. You'll get hot-off-the-press Gold Eagle books, never before published. Send back this card and we'll send you the books and gift you may qualify for absolutely free!

3. And afterward, unless you tell us otherwise, we'll send you five action-packed books every other month to preview (two Mack Bolans, and one each of Able Team, Phoenix Force and Vietnam: Ground Zero). If you decide to keep them, you'll pay only $2.49 per book—16% less than the suggested retail cover price for five books—and that's it! There's NO extra charge for postage and handling.

4. You must be completely satisfied, or you may return a shipment of books, at our cost or cancel at any time simply by noting so on your shipping statement.

FREE SURPRISE MYSTERY GIFT
IT COULD BE YOURS FREE WHEN YOU PLAY "LUCKY 7".

PLAY "LUCKY 7"

Just scratch off the silver area above with a coin.
Then check below to see which gifts you get.

YES! I have scratched off the silver area above. Rush me any Free Books and Free Surprise Gift I may have won. I understand that I am under no obligation to purchase any books. I may keep these free gifts and return my statement marked "cancel." If I do not cancel, then send me my 5 brand-new Gold Eagle novels every second month as they come off the presses. Bill me at the low price of $2.49 for each book—a saving of 16% off the total suggested retail cover price for five books. There is NO extra charge for postage and handling. I can always return a shipment, at your cost, or cancel at any time. The Free Books and Surprise Gift remain mine to keep forever.

165 CIM RAA9

NAME _____

ADDRESS _____ Apt No _____

CITY _____ STATE _____ ZIP CODE _____

7 7 7	WORTH FOUR FREE BOOKS AND FREE SURPRISE GIFT
🍒 🍒 🍒	WORTH FOUR FREE BOOKS
● ● ●	WORTH THREE FREE BOOKS
🔔 🔔 🍒	WORTH TWO FREE BOOKS

Offer limited to one per household and not valid to present subscribers. Terms and prices subject to change without notice. Iowa and NY residents subject to sales tax.

PRINTED IN U.S.A.

© 1989 GOLD EAGLE

Colicci was punched into the air, his body penetrated by a hundred steel balls, each one like a small bullet. He fell to the ground like a bloody rag.

Bolan and Shondor had thrown themselves away from the grenade, so that the bodies of the automobiles were between them and the explosion.

Two men dressed in khaki pants and checkered wool shirts barreled out of the door of the motel room, both carrying AK-47s. They stood just outside the door and loosed long bursts at the parked cars.

The vehicles shook under the impact. Glass flew, and slugs broke through sheet steel and shredded the interiors. But Bolan and Shondor were pressed to the rear of the cars, protected by the engines and frames.

The Executioner rolled off the back of the Pontiac and crouched to take aim. One of the hardmen spotted him and jerked the muzzle of his assault rifle into target acquisition. But Bolan fired first.

The single silenced shot from the Beretta ripped into the man's upper abdomen, and he dropped to his knees before sprawling on his face.

Shondor, recklessly ignoring the sweeping gunfire from the other hardman, had rolled into the clear and lay on his belly, firing rapidly. His fourth shot caught the hardman in the hip and spun him around before Bolan could yell at him to cease fire. The warrior saw the man's body jerk from the shock of a slug, and he knew he'd never get to question him.

THE SHERIFF of Inyo County studied Shondor's Justice Department credentials then gravely accepted the introduction to Colonel Pollock.

"Those two'd just be hired guns," the sheriff said when the Bureau at Sacramento returned the identifications established by the faxed fingerprints taken from the two bodies. "Criminal records—suspected of a lot of stuff never proved. Bet you'd like to know who hired 'em."

"That's the question," Bolan replied.

"Well, Colonel, we'll keep workin' on it, but I can't promise you we'll ever find out."

7

Jasmin Malik sat staring at a map of California. Kirchner had hired a pair of local gunmen and tried to kill Bolan in some village out there. The German had read a news story about radioactivity in the water of a lake near the Los Angeles water system and, supposing Bolan would come to investigate, had hired two unskillful American hit men to attempt to blast him out with grenades.

Kirchner now sat at dinner with Napoleon Malik in a fine Cairo restaurant, explaining what had happened while she, a woman, was excluded from the meeting and the discussion.

Malik wanted her near when he felt threatened—she had saved him more than once. But when he felt secure, as he usually did in Cairo, she could stay in the hotel and take a meal from room service. Because she was a woman.

Someday she would use one of those weapons Malik thought she used exceptionally well and would put a 9 mm bullet into his belly. Because she was a woman.

There was nothing of interest on Cairo television so she rose to switch off the set. She stood too abruptly, and for an instant she stiffened and grimaced with pain. The scars on her back never quite stopped hurting. The damaged flesh hadn't healed right. It was as though she didn't have enough skin to cover her back, and when she pulled against it, it tightened in a ferocious pang.

Every time it happened she relived the hour...

They had brought her from the jail in heavy chains, shackles on her legs, manacles on her wrists. She had staggered into the dusty forecourt of the mosque, stumbling, weak with terror. Islamic law prevailed in Pakistan since the murder of Bhutto. They might have amputated a hand or a foot, except that they could find nothing in the Koran that specified the penalty for selling hashish. So instead, "mercifully," as they insisted, she would receive a hundred stripes.

That was the term, and those were the words of her sentence—"one hundred stripes."

The court of mullahs had imposed the sentence, then confessed they didn't quite know how to execute it. Maybe they knew how in Karachi. In Lahore no one knew exactly how to carry out the punishment prescribed by the revived Islamic law.

No great problem. While she lay in a stone-bound cell behind thick old wrought iron bars, dreading the punishment she doubted she could survive, an army van had arrived—the traveling executioners come to cut off hands and feet and to administer vigorous floggings.

In the bright sunlight of the forecourt, before an approving crowd, she was forced to her knees in front of a thick post newly set in the earth. By law, men received their stripes standing, and women took theirs kneeling. The law provided, too, that she wasn't to be exposed naked to the crowd. Not until she had been forced to embrace the post like a lover, her handcuffs run through a ring on the far side, and a heavy belt had strapped her body tight against the sunwarmed wood, were her clothes torn away, exposing just her back and buttocks, which were to receive the punishment.

Someday, she was determined, she would return to murder the men who had pronounced judgment—the mullahs of Lahore. One of them stood in front of her and read her sentence before the lashing began, intoning every unctuous syllable with conspicuous pleasure.

Then it began. The first stroke, across the middle of her back, made her throw her head hard against the post. The pain was like fire, like being stroked with a red-hot poker, except that it whistled through the air and struck with an excruciating shock that knocked the breath out of her. And that was just the first.

She had been determined not to cry out, not to give them the satisfaction of hearing her scream. But before the fifth lash not only was she shrieking in agony, she was begging them to stop.

Whatever satisfaction the mullahs of Lahore had wanted, they got—in full measure. She was reduced to a screaming, writhing animal, unable even to beg.

But as God was merciful, so was the law. Sometime, somewhere short of the hundred stripes—she never knew just how many she had taken—they stopped. The law said that no one was to be flogged to death. She had taken perhaps half her punishment, and now she would be returned to jail. When she had healed, she would be brought to the stake again, and the punishment would be completed. That was the law.

Napoleon Malik had been in the crowd and seen her punishment. He had liked what he had seen for reasons unworthy of any man, and he had offered the jailer a price—a bribe—for her release.

It was difficult to transfer to Mack Bolan her enduring hatred of the mullahs of Lahore, but she did—a part of that hate, at least. She had never met the man. She knew of him only what she had heard and read. But she knew Mack Bolan, the Executioner, was a man in a way that Napoleon Malik could never be, that Kirchner could never be, that no man she knew had ever been—and a man was what had injured her. She would have her revenge on the mullahs someday, and someday she would drop Malik to his knees in a short imitation of what he had seen her endure, and had enjoyed; but for the moment she would take this Bolan, this Executioner, for part of her revenge. It was odd how much she could hate him without ever having met him.

And he was the key. He would turn up wherever they tried to use their radioactive materials, and would do what none of the governments dared do.

ALBRECHT KIRCHNER was mesmerized by the belly dancer who worked on a small stage at the front of the room.

The German was fat and sweaty, a typical European in Cairo, wearing a white suit, fascinated with his brief and touristic look at another civilization, as he supposed.

"A quick try," he said to Malik, referring to the gunplay in Los Angeles. "Nothing much ventured."

Malik sipped the wine that was forbidden him as a Muslim in a Muslim country. "Very well," he replied. "But another attempt must be better done."

"And successful."

"I may point out to you that many others have tried."

"I know. I have lost friends to this man. Putting him underground will be sweet."

"The effort cannot be clumsy, not amateurish," Malik said pointedly.

Kirchner shrugged. "You mean the California thing. It was an opportunity to catch him off guard. Little was invested. And if it had worked—"

"It is behind us." Malik dismissed the subject. "Now we have two problems, not just one."

"Dihanesi also," said Kirchner. "A believer."

"Hojatolislam Hajan Dihanesi," said Malik, using the Iranian's religious title. Dihanesi was a Muslim religious leader, a rank below an ayatollah. "He is indeed a believer. And he has his followers in the Islamic Strike Force."

"Your leadership is threatened?" Kirchner asked.

"My leadership is doomed," Malik replied. "You and I are of the old school, Kirchner. We are about to be replaced by a new generation. A generation of fanatics. Men like Dihanesi care nothing about—" he raised his wineglass "—about many things that are important to you and me. You and I have lived well off being fighters for the freedom of oppressed people."

"I had to learn what is important."

"But you did," Malik said. "You learned that being in the Baader-Meinhof gang, being ever hunted . . . well, you learned a man can't live many years sustained only by the satisfaction from killing and destroying. So your friends are dead, and you live well. As I do. But there's no room for us among the fanatics."

"What are you driving at?" Kirchner asked.

"We might be able to save our leadership by achieving a great triumph."

"Like forcing the United States and the Western European powers to their knees?" Kirchner suggested.

"No. Only the fanatics believe we can do that. *You* don't believe it Albrecht. You never did. You know very well that if we wipe out a city, the imperialists—as we like to call them—will wipe out *five* cities. Perhaps Tehran, Tripoli, Damascus, Sidi . . . maybe Baghdad, Riyadh, even Mecca. Terror can achieve only so much, my friend. Then the powerful nations strike back—senselessly, like wounded dogs. And they destroy the weak. Utterly. And we are the weak. In the bitter end, Albrecht, the oppressed are the oppressed because they are the weak."

"And what you are saying, I suppose, leads to a conclusion," Kirchner said dryly.

"It does. The death of Bolan would be a triumph. Enough to save us for a time. I tell you, though, we do not dare poison half the population of the city of Los Angeles, which is what we are looking at now. I think another demonstration somewhere. And dispose of Bolan. And we will have saved ourselves."

Kirchner leaned back in his chair and used a lighter to light a long, thick cigar. "Do I detect another idea behind this?"

"Of course you do. Suppose we mount another demonstration, this one successful, and then secretly suggest to the government of the United States that some nice round sum, say one billion dollars, paid into the right accounts, would purchase our peace."

"Would pay for our retirement," Kirchner said.

Malik nodded. "Precisely. Yours and mine. And Balbo Manero's, I suppose, since the Red Brigades are in hiding. A few others. A retirement secure against the fury of the Dihanesis of the world." Malik shrugged. "If we can't reform the world to our liking, at least we can arrange to enjoy it."

Kirchner smiled. "I've often wondered just how I would live in a world reformed according to the prescriptions of what we have called the United Righteous—or, for that matter, a world reformed as Baader-Meinhof would have arranged it."

"So. We begin to see the dimensions of what we have to do, don't we?"

Kirchner blew a thick cloud of cigar smoke toward the ceiling. "First, Bolan," he said. "I accept responsibility for that."

SHONDOR SAVACHEVA was hospitalized in Sacramento, after being flown out by helicopter. Bolan went with him and stayed at the hospital until he learned that Shondor's wound wouldn't cripple him and he'd be permitted to leave the hospital in a few days.

Bolan contacted Brognola.

"What I want to know," the big Fed growled, "is how the hell they knew where to find you. Was the whole thing a setup? Sounds like somebody dumped a little radioactive material into the lake to lure you out there and take a shot at you."

"They weren't that smart. If they had been, they'd have taken me out with a rifle while I was walking around the lake. It reads like a quick and dirty."

"Okay," said Brognola. "But somebody knew you were there. It confirms what you saw on the videotape. Getting you is one of the objectives of the United Righteous."

"What's the word?" Bolan asked.

"Nothing about any stuff moving in the States. It's as if your job in West Virginia cooled them—for a while, anyway. I think there's something brewing in Europe. Let me get back to you on it."

"Okay. Meanwhile, I think I'll go to San Francisco and pay my respects to Frank Colicci's family."

HE ARRIVED TOO LATE for the funeral, which was held in the morning, so he went to the house in the afternoon to speak to the dead agent's wife. Linda Colicci gratefully accepted his assurance that her husband had died in the service of his country.

As he was about to leave, Bolan felt a light touch on his arm.

"Excuse me."

He turned and found himself facing an extraordinarily beautiful young woman.

"Colonel Pollock, right?"

Bolan frowned and nodded.

"My name's Debra Crowell. I'm a friend of Linda's. We went to school together."

When he didn't respond, she went on.

"They were deeply in love. He was a good man, Colonel Pollock."

Bolan nodded. "I felt I had to come to tell her he didn't die for nothing."

"She never really thought he did. But it must have meant a lot to her to have you come to talk to her. I wish I could stay with her longer, but I came up from L.A. for just a day or two. I, uh, I love San Francisco. Wish I were here in different circumstances. Have you been here before?"

He nodded. "Sure. On business a number of times."

"You like good Chinese food?" she asked.

"Yes. I do."

"I know a good restaurant, if you're interested...."

THEY WALKED TO A SMALL PLACE several blocks away, and the food *was* good. It was brought to their table on a succession of wheeled tables, from which small portions of a wide variety of dishes were offered. Even for a steak-and-potatoes man who wasn't particularly in a mood to appreciate a meal, this was delicious.

"Colonel Pollock," Debra began. "Colonel. I guess that means you're not an FBI man as Frank was."

"Right. And I'm not really a colonel, either. I'm retired."

She smiled playfully. "At your age? You certainly don't look the part of the retired officer."

"In and out young," he replied.

She laughed lightly. "Maybe you'll forgive my saying this, but I don't think you're telling the truth, exactly. You were with Frank when he was killed. The news stories say another man was wounded, plus the two hit men were killed. They threw grenades. It sounds like one hell of a shootout."

Bolan waited to see where the woman was leading.

"I think you're some kind of secret agent," Debra stated baldly.

"If I was, I obviously couldn't tell you, could I?"

"You don't want to talk about it. I understand. But let me tell you something. I know a bit about what you're doing. I mean, I know about the stolen radioactive material and the threats that have been made."

Once more Bolan remained silent, letting her talk.

"Look, Colonel. What you told Linda Colicci this afternoon didn't come as any great surprise to her. Frank wasn't supposed to confide in his wife, but he did, and Linda confided in me after he was killed. So I know he was helping you fight a gang of terrorists who want to do on a big scale what was done on a small scale in Palma, Majorca. And I know something more than that. In fact, I think I know something you don't know, and I think you'd better."

"Okay. Tell me."

"I work for a lab in Los Angeles," she said. "I'm almost certain we're missing some cesium 137. I have a suspicion the owner of the company sold it, but he's covering up the sale. I'm afraid to think of who might have it and what they might be planning to do with it. Suppose it was dumped in an aqueduct."

"Have you told this to anybody else?" Bolan asked.

She shook her head. "It wasn't until Linda told me what Frank had told her that I began to put two and two together. I mean, I knew about Majorca. Everybody in the world knows what happened there. I didn't know anything like that had come to the States. I'd figured until then that my boss had just sold the stuff to get the money."

"Maybe he did."

"No. Our inventory shows it's still in the lab. But it isn't. What's more, a legal sale of the stuff would have to be to somebody with a license to have it, and we'd have a record of that sale, with the license number and all." She shook her head again. "It's just gone."

"Who knows this besides you?"

"I don't know. Maybe just me, plus the boss."

He stared thoughtfully at Debra for a moment. She'd said what she had to say and now turned her attention to her dinner. "How much cesium is missing?" he asked.

"More than what was put into those swimming pools. Enough to create a disaster."

"So why did you come to me? You want me to go to L.A. and look into the deal?"

"I thought you might."

"Tomorrow," he replied.

"Not so fast, Colonel. I can't go back until Monday. I took the rest of the week off. I mean, this is Friday, and the lab is closed weekends. I can't get you in over the weekend. When I leave the lab Monday afternoon, I'll carry out the keys. Monday night, we can go in and make sure the cesium is missing. I promise you it is, but we can double check."

"Maybe somebody else should be handling this."

Debra shrugged. "I'm not going to tell just *anybody*. But look, we can go to L.A. in the morning. What's wrong with putting in a little time on the beach? You can probably find some way to amuse yourself on a weekend in Los Angeles, particularly if I help you. Then Monday..."

"I've got a call to make first, but you've got a deal."

"WHAT'S THE NAME of this lab?" Hal Brognola asked when Bolan reached him on the telephone a little after midnight.

"Redondo Equipment and Supplies. She says it's in Santa Monica."

"I don't have any other firm leads that demand your attention," Brognola told him. "Why don't you check that one out? Let me know what's going on."

BOLAN FLEW to Los Angeles with Debra Crowell. He took a motel room in Santa Monica, and she said she'd join him in the afternoon. They could spend some time on the beach, then maybe have dinner somewhere.

In a white satin bikini, she was spectacular. He swam in the surf, but she did not go near the water. When he returned and sat down beside her, she told him more about Redondo Equipment.

"My boss," she began, later, "is the owner. I think he's got a partner, but I don't know for sure. His name is Alfred Macy. To be frank, I think his name's really Alfredo and the Macy is short for something else. Anyway, the company is in the business of selling hospital and doctor's-office equipment, X-ray machines for dentists and chemicals. No prescription drugs."

Bolan had received a call from Brognola around mid-morning. The big Fed confirmed the existence of a company by the name Redondo Equipment and Supplies in Santa Monica. As well, the Justice Department check had identified the president of the company as one Alfred Maesi, a.k.a. Macy.

The next day, Sunday, Bolan rented a car and drove by the headquarters of Redondo Equipment. The place was deserted, as Debra had said it would be. The structure was a concrete-block building painted light yellow, two stories in front, one story behind. Three delivery vans bearing the name of the company were parked along one side. Nothing unusual. Redondo was a small business with a specialized line.

Debra showed up at the motel on Sunday afternoon and they discussed their after-hours probe of the offices of Redondo Equipment and Supplies.

"I'll have all the keys," she told him. "There's no watchman. A security service checks the building four times a night. If we watch for them, we can go in, do the job and be out long before they come back."

"No alarm system?"

"Not if you get in with a key."

"And the safe where the cesium is kept can be opened with a key, too?"

"Yes. It's not a safe. It's a lead-lined strong room. The radioactive material in there is kept in lead containers, and no radioactivity is supposed to escape. Even if it does, the danger is confined inside the room. If you spilled something, you could get out and slam the door."

"If all that has to be done is go inside that room and look for the container of cesium, I don't see just what my part in this is," Bolan said. "Why don't you just walk in during the day and see if the cesium is missing?"

"I'm not authorized to go in there. If I went in during the day, they'd see me. The door to the room is in the middle of a work area. So it has to be done at night. And...well, I say it ought to be easy, but if anything went wrong...I'm nervous about this. Scared, if you want to know the truth. If my boss sold that stuff to the wrong people, this could be a rough deal."

"All right," he said. "What time do you have in mind?"

"Let's say ten o'clock."

BOLAN ARMED HIMSELF for the probe. If he encountered any trouble, the silenced Beretta 93-R would probably serve better than the big .44 Magnum Desert Eagle. He decided to wear casual clothes—a lightweight dark blue jacket and jeans. The jacket concealed the holster that housed the Beretta and a sheath in which he carried a short knife.

Just before he left the room he took from his luggage a weapon that Shondor had given him in the helicopter ambulance on the way to the hospital in Sacramento. "They'll find this before they take me into surgery," he said. "And it's just as well they don't."

What he had handed over was a Baby Browning, a 6.35 mm automatic, only four inches long and weighing less than ten ounces.

The interesting part was the holster. Suspended by a thin belt around the hips under a man's clothes, it hung the pistol snugly in his crotch. To get it out, a man had to unzip his pants and reach in for it. The idea was that rarely when a man was frisked would anyone press a hand up there, and the weapon would go undetected to all but the most thorough search.

On impulse Bolan took off his clothes and strapped on the soft leather holster. He hung the Browning in place and dressed again. It was true that the pistol was absolutely invisible, in a place where hardly anyone was likely to grope for it.

He picked up Debra at her apartment. They arrived at Redondo Equipment a little after ten, parked across the street and waited for the security company to come by to check the place.

They had half an hour to wait. It was ten-thirty before the Ford marked with the logo of the security company pulled up in front of the building and two uniformed men got out and went in. They left the building five minutes later and drove away.

Bolan and Debra left the car parked across the street and walked over to the building. Without a word she unlocked the front door, and they entered a small reception room. She put her hands on his shoulders to tell him to stand just where he was until she opened a box and used another key to turn off the security system.

"Okay," she whispered. "The offices are in this part of the building. The strong room is in back."

Leaving the reception room, they passed through a door into a short hallway, then through another door and into a work area.

The big room wasn't lighted, but enough light entered through the windows—moonlight, the glare of headlights and the neon tubing of other businesses—to give him a clear view. It was a room where shipments were boxed. A forklift truck stacked with boxes was parked near a big sliding door. One table seemed to be used for assembling cartons, another for taping them shut. Bins of packing materials stood nearby.

"Through here."

Debra led the way into a larger room behind the first that had the look of an industrial laboratory. It was equipped with glassware, sinks, racks of bottles, burners, scales. Bolan's first impression was that it looked like too many of the labs he had seen where opium base was refined into heroin, or where cocaine was produced from raw coca, and for a moment he wondered if she had brought him into the middle of a large-scale narcotics operation. But it wasn't that. The chemicals were too many and too varied. It looked legitimate.

"Over there." She pointed to a door.

The single door was different, metal and locked. It was what she'd said, a strong room.

"Wait a minute," Debra cautioned.

She stepped to a lab table and picked up a Geiger counter.

Bolan saw her switch on the counter, then didn't see anything more. A bolt of lightning exploded in his head.

WHEN THE BLINDING light was gone and darkness returned, his first awareness was of a throbbing ache in his head.

He'd been coldcocked.

The warrior didn't open his eyes. He tried to get some kind of orientation from feeling and hearing and found that he was lying on his side on the floor. Someone was talking.

"No, dammit! I want to know who he is. These documents . . . Colonel Rance Pollock. If he *is* Colonel Rance Pollock, then we have the wrong man."

"We have to kill him anyway."

"Not, I'm telling you, until we find out who he is!"

"And how do you plan to find out?"

"The easy way. Prepare a syringe."

Very slowly, careful not to let them see the motion, Bolan pressed his arm to his side. The Beretta was gone. So was the knife . . . but the baby Browning was still in place. He could feel it.

He'd have to make his move before they got their syringe loaded. He opened his eyes.

"Aha. So, Colonel Pollock. You have returned."

At first he had difficulty focusing on them. There were three men. Debra was nowhere in sight.

Two of the men, if he could judge, were Americans, one with a bushy mustache, one with a close-cropped beard.

Hardmen. The third man looked like a European—he spoke with a trace of accent. Maybe German.

"Do you want to tell us your real name?" the maybe-German asked.

"What's wrong with Pollock?" Bolan groaned. He rolled over and sat up painfully. "My family liked it."

"Yes," the man mused. "Pollock. I don't think so. I think you're somebody else. Do you want to tell us?"

Bolan glanced from one man to the other, judging all three as best he could. "You mind if I stand up?"

"If you can," said the maybe-German. "But—" he drew a pistol, an old Walther, WW II vintage "—don't try to move against us. We think we know who you are, and it makes us nervous."

Bolan had to struggle to reach his feet. His head ached badly, and he was dizzy. But he knew he had to overcome dizziness if he was to have any chance of doing anything. He grabbed a table for support and tried to make the room stop spinning.

The man with the mustache faced him with a pistol while the third was busy filling a syringe from a small bottle.

"Colonel," said the man with the accent, "we are going to interrogate you. Yes? You see, we are going to inject you with that which will bring the truth out of you. That is, unless you want to tell us the truth voluntarily."

Bolan sucked in and blew out a deep breath. "Tell you what," he muttered. "Let me go to the bathroom before I wet my pants, and then we can talk about it."

"Yes," the European agreed, "and put some cold water on your face." He nodded at the man with the pistol. "You go with him. Keep a careful watch."

As he stumbled toward the bathroom—exaggerating the movement—Bolan looked around for Debra. She wasn't there. They were going to kill him after they tried to find out who he was, and maybe they had already killed her. For a supply of cesium 137 . . .

"Be quick about it," his guard said as he pulled open the door into a washroom.

Bolan stepped to the urinal. The man stood in the doorway behind him, keeping his revolver leveled on his back. The baby Browning was there, warm from contact with his body.

He urinated to let the gunner think that was the true purpose of his visit. He couldn't look back to see if the man was any less alert or had lowered the muzzle of his weapon so much as an inch. Whatever the man was doing, Bolan knew he had no options, would have no second chance. He could almost palm the little automatic, out of sight in his hand.

Bolan turned slowly. The man was smirking.

"Feel better?"

At the last possible instant, the gunner spotted the Browning, but for him it was too late. Bolan had by then thrust it upward, and as the warrior fired he threw himself against the man, sending slugs up into his heart and lungs. The hardman stiffened and staggered backward. But he was in Bolan's clutch, and the pistol was out beside the Executioner, almost behind his back.

Bolan grabbed for the pistol and wrenched it from the man's hand. It was a Smith & Wesson .357 Magnum, and Bolan transferred it quickly to his right hand.

The European fired his Walther—and hit the man with the mustache squarely in the middle of the back.

Bolan needed just one shot from the .357 to throw the new arrival on his back across one of the lab tables, shattering glassware, causing a brief puff of smoke as two chemicals mixed.

The bearded man who had been filling the syringe had run at the sound of the first shots. By the time Bolan could turn toward him, he was running through a door at the rear of the lab. The warrior gave chase, but by the time he reached the door, the bearded man had run out of the building.

Bolan retraced his steps and began to search for Debra.

8

"There was no Debra Crowell," said Hal Brognola, who had flown to Los Angeles to confer with the police and discourage their initial determination to find the man who killed two men in the Redondo Equipment lab. "You were had, big guy."

"It was a setup."

"A setup to kill you," Brognola affirmed. "There was no cesium in that lab, ever. Alfred Macy is an honest guy. He's been checked out by LAPD and the FBI."

Bolan stood at the window in his motel room, staring across the highway at the misty beach, the crashing breakers that came out of the fog from an invisible ocean.

"She was good."

"I figure that up by Mono Lake you were shot at by the second team," Brognola went on. "But the first team knew you were in California and watched to see where you went. It was easy enough for her to make up her story that she was a friend of Linda Colicci. She knew you'd never check that out—though we've had to, now. She and her buddies had a story made up to use, about some missing cesium 137. They knew you'd be interested in that."

"And the weekend," Bolan said, "her insistence we couldn't move until Monday night—"

"Gave her buddies time to set the deal up," Brognola finished for him. "They had to case the building, figure out the alarm system, get the keys—"

"How'd they get the keys?"

"Bought them," the big Fed replied. "For a hell of a price on Saturday afternoon. They promised the man who sold them—the lab manager—they'd make no mess. There'd be no way to identify him. They'd bring him his keys back. And so on."

"Who were they?" Bolan asked.

"The German was named Dieter Hesse, an old Baader-Meinhof type. Spent four years in a West German prison. He's been out of sight for a long time. The other man, the one with the big mustache, we haven't been able to identify yet. His fingerprints aren't on record anywhere. He doesn't seem to be wanted or reported missing. We don't know who he might have been."

Bolan blew out a noisy breath. "So, okay. Who *was* the girl?"

"LAPD got a set of prints on her. The Germans and Interpol have given us a full rundown on your friend 'Debra Crowell'—a damned smart and dangerous operator. A real pro."

Bolan shook his head. His eyes remained fixed on the beach, on beach boys determined to carry their boards into the surf in spite of the fog and chill. "Maybe so," he replied, "but I feel like a fool."

"You aren't the first man who's been taken in by a pretty girl, and not the first one taken in by *her*, either."

"Fill me in on her."

"Her real name is Ilse von der Schulenberg," Brognola said. "Debra Crowell was only one of many names she's used over the years. Her father is a stockbroker in Hamburg. Her mother is a concert pianist—not a very good one, the Germans say. Neither of her parents know where she is, apparently, or care. She became pregnant and had an abortion when she was fourteen. The man who got her pregnant was a university professor, something of a neo-Nazi, the reports say. He was shot to death with his own pistol about a year after Ilse had the abortion. She was the chief suspect and was held for a while, but she was still only fifteen years old and they didn't have a case against her. They had to let her go."

"Nice girl."

Brognola grinned and shrugged. "She was the kind they liked in the Baader-Meinhof gang. She had little education, and she hated her family. She hated the world. She made a good recruit, a gullible soldier in a cynical army. She was recruited by Heinrich Kröller, who had made her a pet as well as a soldier."

"Kröller?"

"Yeah, that Kröller. You met him."

"He came close to taking me out."

"Don't I remember," the big Fed replied. "Anyway, Kröller got himself shot, too. It's generally understood little Ilse killed him, but for that she wasn't even arrested. The Germans didn't give a damn who killed Heinrich Kröller, just as long as somebody did."

"I don't suppose they had a case against her," Bolan said dryly.

"No evidence. The girl is either innocent and always falsely accused, or else she covers her tracks like a cool, calm expert."

"I could have sworn she was an American."

"I imagine," Brognola replied. "That's a part of her thing—she's an actress. Some people think Babette Mercier was Ilse von der Schulenberg."

"The woman who hired the man to try to hit Mitterand?"

"Right, Gaulier. Tried to kill the president of France. Remember, he insisted it was all Babette's idea? Well, Babette may have been Ilse."

"A dangerous woman."

"Yes, and there's another element to her reputation. They say she never forgives. You represent a failure on her record, and *that* she will never forgive."

"I wonder if the guys she's working with will forgive her," Bolan mused.

ILSE WAS FIDGETY while waiting for her luggage to be examined at Frankfurt Airport—Fritz Hausser waiting for her.

She had spent the past year in the United States, using a phony Swiss passport, and had been called home when she had to report that Colonel Rance Pollock, who was almost certainly Mack Bolan, had escaped the trap she had so carefully laid for him.

"It wasn't my fault," she complained when they were in the car and on their way into the city. "I delivered him to Hesse. They knocked him unconscious, and when I left, he was disarmed and lying on the floor."

"It's history," Hausser replied. "Anyway, Reynolds called, too. He reported how it happened. You did your part. No one has any criticism of you."

Encouraged, she took a bolder line. "I did a smart job, Fritz. How Hesse managed to screw it up—"

"Bolan had a small gun hidden on him. *You* didn't find it, either. You were there when he was searched. Everyone is satisfied you did your job well enough. But I wouldn't press the point, Ilse."

"Albrecht?"

"You'll see him this evening."

She dressed for dinner, knowing that Albrecht Kirchner would expect something revealing. He had become something of a sybarite in recent years. She had been told repeatedly that in the old days of Baader-Meinhof, Albrecht Kirchner had been a lean, angry leader. Now he wanted to enjoy life, while still doing the only thing he knew how to do—trying to make revolution.

That, she reflected—her mind turning in the American way—was a damned odd way to make a living.

But he smoked a big cigar, and they drank champagne, and he said he didn't hold her responsible for the failure in Los Angeles. Obviously, too, he appreciated her red dress, which exposed her shoulders and most of her breasts, plus her legs below a short skirt.

"But we can't fail again, Ilse," he said. "We're being pressed from the rear."

"You used to press from the rear yourself." She spoke with a smile meant to take all but a little of the sting out of the comment.

"You, too, pressed, once," he replied without anger.

She was thirty-one years old. The way she saw it, the battle was lost before she got a chance to fight. *His* generation had failed. Hers had never had a chance. But maybe it would, yet.

"Apart from killing Bolan, what are we about?" she asked.

"Well, we have problems we must address *now*."

"The United Righteous," she said.

He looked at her quizzically, as if surprised that she should have guessed what he had in mind. "Yes. The revolutionary people have one thing in mind. The Islamic fundamentalists have another. We—I mean, we the revolutionaries—have always had our ways of applying pressure and have hoped to achieve our purposes without blowing up the world. But if you believe that this world is but a temporary abode and that a sublime new world awaits you beyond the grave, your values are different."

"Specifically?"

"Malik is losing command of the Islamic Strike Force, just as Arafat once lost control of the PLO. The young men and the believers don't like his patience, which they call cowardice. They've heard of his way of life and don't like that, either. The ISF is our source of two important things—soldiers and money."

"Money from General Laqiya," she said.

"Exactly. His copper and barium profits. He is much more generous with his fellow Muslims than he would be with us. Now, as to soldiers, Hesse and his like have to be paid. The Arab fanatics don't."

"But if they're out of control—"

Kirchner interrupted. "We need two successes," he said. "One, we need to rid ourselves of Bolan. Two, we need a demonstration that will produce some immediate dramatic concession. We're going to have both."

"I would like another crack at Bolan," she stated.

"He knows you now. You can't—"

"I can do it another way. In any case, it will be my risk. I know a little something about the man—at least what he looks like. All I want to know is where he is."

"In a day or two I'll know where he's going to be," Kirchner promised.

ILSE LAID HER PLAN.

Bolan would come to the Rhine playing Colonel Pollock just as she'd be playing Madeleine Dallas. And they'd meet again.

Only he wouldn't know her.

It was easy to change her appearance. Her eyes were blue, and contact lenses could make them violet or green or, as in this case, brown. A technician in a Frankfurt beauty shop dyed her hair dark brown, then cut it short and stiffened it so that it stood erect on top of her head, looking like a dark-brown scrub brush—very stylish. She darkened her eyebrows with a brown cosmetic pencil and her lashes with mascara. She applied vivid brownish-red lipstick.

For a test she asked Fritz Hausser to meet her at the fountain in the center of a covered shopping mall. He didn't know her.

She had no problem with her weapon, which was a fine hunting rifle of Belgian manufacture, modified by a gunsmith. The basic rifle was what Americans had once called a "varmint rifle"—small-caliber, high-velocity, exceptionally accurate. The gunsmith had shortened the barrel and cut away the stock, machining the rifle to accept a stock of steel tubing. It was fitted with a custom silencer and also with a telescopic sight, although she expected to fire from a close enough range to hit her target cleanly without the scope.

The bullets were of the explosive type—meaning that the bullet would be split open on impact so that a wildly deformed bullet would go through flesh. At high velocity. No one had ever survived a chest shot from one of these bullets.

Ilse formed no great personal attachments to people or things, but she loved this rifle. It was something like a cat or dog for her. Sometimes when she had no particular use for it, she would just take it out and look at it—assemble it, disassemble it, assemble it again and peer down the sights. She'd taken something of a risk in keeping it after it had been used. It would have been a difficult possession to explain.

She packed it in her gray BMW and would soon drive south to Mannheim, Karlsruhe, Offenburg. Bolan would arrive in a day or so. She could be certain of that.

HAJAN DIHANESI WAS uncomfortable. To travel in Europe incognito, he'd had to adopt European dress. What was more, he'd had to live a little like Europeans, appearing to tolerate their shameful transgressions against the clearly revealed laws of God.

There was no redeeming these Europeans. He knew that. Not in his lifetime, anyway. The word of the Prophet was but rarely listened to in the cities of Europe or America. A time might come when, in the fullness of his wisdom, God would enlighten all the world. For now, the mission of the faithful had to be the liberation of God's people from the despotic burden of imperialism. More couldn't be accomplished in this generation.

In prayer he had sought guidance about the alliance he had led his men into—an alliance with evil. It was disgusting. *They* were disgusting. Still, they were shrewd, with the shrewdness of Satan, and skilled in all the evils they called technology. What was more, they spoke the languages of the imperialists and could move among them without attracting notice.

If victory was won, even in alliance with Satan, was it not still God's victory? Men whose advice he respected answered yes.

It was then probably the will of God that he continue in this unholy alliance as long as need be to achieve a great victory.

And a great victory was perhaps at hand.

This place where he found himself was a monument to the folly of the French. It was a mammoth hole in the earth, dug out many years ago. The walls of the hole were old concrete, wet and flaking. So was the ceiling. This hole was joined to another by a deep tunnel, part of a vast network of holes and tunnels. In some, though not in this one, ancient guns still faced the river, decades-silent and red with scaly rust.

The river, which could be seen from the slits made for the gun barrels, flowed by, broad and peaceful. It was the boundary between two of the imperialist countries.

Dihanesi had no knowledge of the animosities that had caused the French to dig these holes and tunnels and fill them with weapons and supplies of war. He cared nothing about the shameful history of the imperialists. The words by which they called these fortifications were interesting. They called it the Maginot Line.

Across that river was the land of the German imperialists. On this side, the land of the French imperialists. And they hated each other and had dug these holes and put these guns down here so the French could fire on the Germans if they tried to cross that river.

And this hole the French had dug was an ideal spot for handling the dangerous material that was to be put into the river.

Some of these holes had been made monuments, he was told, monuments to the impious perfidy of the French and Germans. Others, like this one, were abandoned. It was on a remote site on the western bank of the big river, and for ten days now Napoleon Malik had been accumulating the poison in this hole.

Dihanesi had gone down once, just for a moment, to see what they were doing. He hadn't stayed, because they said it was dangerous. They had machines down there, robots. Men in another hole watched the robots on television screens and directed them at their work of receiving materials in small quantities, carried in simple passenger cars and pouring it all together in a big tank.

There, truly, was Satan—in that tank. And shortly they would unleash him on the imperialists.

NAPOLEON MALIK, with Jasmin at his side, walked alongside the swift-flowing gray water of the Rhine. Both of them were fascinated and always would be at the immense quantity of cool water that slid through the broad valley, the same at all seasons of the year.

It was fortunate that the Rhine was swift. The mixture would travel many miles before anyone knew what was in the water. Yet even when they did, they could do nothing about it.

As always, Jasmin carried the weapons. In a confrontation with the Iranians, which was always possible though not likely, they would have an invaluable advantage—the Iranians probably wouldn't think that the woman would be carrying weapons under her clothes. Today she was dressed modestly, to suit the puritanical Hajan Dihanesi, in a loose robe that nicely concealed a mini-Uzi, as well as a Walther PPK.

And there he was—Hojatolislam Hajan Dihanesi, a mullah, as far as she was concerned, a representative of Islamic justice. Involuntarily she stroked the cool steel of the Uzi that hung on a strap under her robe. His two bodyguards couldn't have saved him had she whipped out that deadly little submachine gun and opened fire.

"Greeting," Malik said. "Greeting in the name of God."

"And to you, greeting," Dihanesi replied. They spoke Arabic.

Hardly could two men have confronted each other with greater scorn, or with more smooth skill for concealing their splenetic contempt.

"And so it happens," Malik commented.

"As you wished."

The Iranian hadn't offered a social comment. He acknowledged that they were going to poison the Rhine in a way that would cause panic and probably many deaths, yet not shattering disaster. It was the final demonstration, Malik had promised, then the elimination of a city the same way Hiroshima and Nagasaki had been eliminated. The imperialists would be brought to their knees.

But for some reason Malik wanted another demonstration.

"You will be satisfied with our victory," Malik told him.

Dihanesi turned and looked at the river. He was not very tall, slender. His gray European suit was too big for him. His black hat covered his head but didn't lend the dignity his turban would have lent. Although he was forty years old, his mustache was straggly, like the mustache of an eighteen-year-old. The gift of his faith in God was a serenity that beamed from him. Anyone who studied his face saw that Hajan Dihanesi wasn't troubled by doubt. He *knew* he was right, that his cause was just. He had long ago put behind him any question about that.

"When?" Dihanesi asked simply.

"Why not now?"

Dihanesi nodded. "Why not?"

MALIK HAD SOME telephone calls to make before the plan was executed. One was to Kirchner, who was in Berlin at the moment. Kirchner telephone Ilse von der Schulenberg. She reached a hill, on the German side, before the pumping began.

She didn't need binoculars. What happened was obvious enough, if you knew where to look, and when.

It was about two in the afternoon. The skies were gray. A few drops of cold rain had already fallen, and the wind and swirling clouds promised more.

From the hills on the German side of the Rhine, crumbling old fortifications of the Maginot Line could be seen. They stretched in both directions—to the Swiss frontier on the south, the Ardennes Forest on the north—following the Rhine until the river turned east into Germany and then following the national frontier north and west. The French nation had poured its treasure into the Line in the twenties and thirties, and in 1940 it hadn't delayed the German tanks a single hour.

But the bunkers were there, and the complex of interconnecting tunnels.

The workmen of the United Righteous had carried the radioactive material and the oil into one of the bunkers, down into the wet concrete-and-steel cavern now populated only by rats. The material, yes, and powerful electric pumps. When all was ready, Ilse would have a ringside seat.

Everyone started to leave—she could see the cars pulling away. Suddenly she heard several muffled thumps. They'd blown up the tunnels, the entrances to the bunker where the pumps and tanks waited.

From outside, someone pulled a switch.

Three thick black streams shot out of the gun slits across the few yards of green grass between the concrete and into the river. The wind caught the streams, lifting little plumes off them, but the leg-thick streams shot fifty yards out over the water and fell into the Rhine River.

Half an hour passed before the first police vehicles arrived at the bunkers. By then the tanks were empty, and the pumps had shut themselves off.

BOLAN AND SHONDOR caught the newspaper story at an all-night truck stop in Arizona. They were on the way to check out a report of another hijacked tanker truck of sludge, in west Texas. Bolan had been driving, and he'd decided he and Shondor were entitled to a big, filling West Texas breakfast. They'd been sitting at the counter when a man came in and started stuffing morning newspapers into the rack. Both of them saw the headline. Bolan grabbed a paper.

Radioactive Oil in Rhine River

The rapidly dispersing black oily slick on the surface of the Rhine has been conclusively identified as being radioactive. All Europe has been conscious of the threat of radioactivity in water since the tragedy of Majorca, and alarm has spread rapidly throughout the Rhine Valley, the industrial heartland of Europe.

The spill occurred on the upper river, and the poisonous slick is moving rapidly downstream on the swift current.

Every boat and ship that can leave the Rhine has left it. The canals and tributaries are now choked with river craft of every type. As the slick approaches, lock doors are closed on the canals. The waterfront on both sides of the river is largely abandoned. Industrial plants that draw water from the river for cooling have been compelled to shut down.

The first major cities affected were Ludwigshafen and Mannheim, where the slick raced through a narrow neck of the river and deposited radioactive sludge on the waterfronts of both. No boats ventured out to measure the radioactivity in the river.

Helicopters hover over the water, lowering radiation counters. Radio and television stations are keeping all

Europe constantly informed of the advance of the poisonous slick down the river.

It will pass Mainz and Wiesbaden in several hours, then swirl through the turns of the so-called "Romantic Rhine," the castle-bordered rapids where in German legend the Lorelei sang and lured boatmen to their death on the rocks. A little farther on it will pass Remagen, where there is no longer a bridge.

As Shondor stood by and made sure no one was listening, Bolan put through a call to Hal Brognola in Virginia.

"Sorry about the hour. Just got the Rhine story," the warrior began. "How many dead?"

"Never mind the hour," the big Fed replied. "Nobody's asleep anywhere. Deaths... actually, not many. The word went out, and people backed away from the river. The Rhine is swift, you know—much swifter than, say, the Mississippi—and the slick is long, thin and moving fast. In some of the bends of the river it's not touching the banks at all. Of course, what it does touch is contaminated."

"And people die," Bolan said grimly.

"Yeah. Some old river people just refuse to leave the boats they've lived on all their lives. There's a story that one old fellow said he'd just use his hose and spray the sludge off his boat as it went by—but he didn't realize the pump that fed his hose was sucking up radioactive water. He's in the hospital. Some policemen are in bad shape. They ran the river boats into the slick, trying to keep other boaters out of it."

"The kind of guys who always get it."

He could hear Brognola blow an unhappy breath. "Right. Some guys put it on the line for other people."

"But not many deaths, huh?"

"Well, not so far. But think of what it's going to do to the economy of Europe. I spent an hour with the President. The industries of at least five countries are shut down for a week. At least. The Rhine is used to transport coal, iron ore, steel, oil. You name it."

"Any big word from the United Righteous?"

"No. They probably figure they don't have to issue a communiqué."

"Is there any way that it could have been an accident?"

"No way, Striker. The damned stuff was pumped into the Rhine out of an abandoned bunker on the Maginot Line. Which brings up a point. Paul Lemaire is asking you to come to Europe."

"We've got problems here," the warrior replied.

"Our President requests your cooperation...."

BOLAN SAW no real point in rushing to Europe. On the other hand he knew that if he'd asked for Paul Lemaire's help, the guy would rush to the States or anywhere else.

Within eighteen hours of the oily radioactive mess being pumped into the Rhine, "Colonel Rance Pollock" landed at Charles DeGaulle Airport in Paris and was flown by French military helicopter to Strasbourg.

Two agents met him and drove him out to the old Maginot Line bunker that had been used to do the job Akada and his thugs had meant to do in West Virginia. There were Lemaire and Heinrich Schumann, of the Intelligence service of the Federal Republic of Germany. He was a tall, strong, dark-haired man, much like Bolan in appearance. He looked anything but Teutonic, and he carried himself with poised self-confidence.

On their way out in the car the two men nearly choked Bolan with their cigarette smoke. Both were chain smokers and were partial to heavy, unfiltered cigarettes. Schumann's voice was ravaged by smoking.

"Mostly it's the plutonium," Lemaire said. "Some strontium. Some radioactive carbons. But nothing of the cesium 137 that was used in Majorca. Highly poisonous, to be sure, but not of the strength that was used in the swimming pools."

"How long were they in the bunker?" Bolan asked. "How long did it take them to prepare the mixture?"

"Not more than a week," Schumann replied. "The quantity introduced into the Rhine was only a fraction of what they planned to introduce into the Ohio River. With no cesium. It's another warning that they can do worse."

Bolan looked at the Rhine. It was much like the Ohio, except that the current was swifter. A mile upstream from where the radioactive oil had been sprayed on the surface, river traffic was heavy, even a little heavier than normal. But police boats guarded the point where the poison was introduced, churning back and forth, displaying flashing blue lights. Downstream from that, only a few boats moved on the water. Helicopters hovered above.

"The people who did this must be long gone," Bolan commented.

"Not all," Lemaire replied. "We know where to find a suspect. In Germany."

"It is a delicate matter," Schumann added.

"Delicate," Lemaire repeated with a trace of scorn in his voice. "If I had the man on *my* side of the river, it wouldn't be a delicate matter. I would—"

"The man is Iranian," Schumann said. "Several agencies have been watching him for some time. He's been in contact with known terrorists in Berlin and Frankfurt and in Athens. His name is Hojatolislam Hajan Dihanesi. Hojatolislam is a religious title. He's a member of the Iranian parliament. We won't touch him unless we know—"

"Know what?" Lemaire interrupted irritably. "All I ask is that you someway herd him back across the Rhine."

"We have him under close surveillance," Schumann said. "It will be particularly interesting to see who visits him."

"So where is he?" Bolan asked.

"In Baden-Baden," Schumann answered. "The old resort where Europeans used to come to bathe in the mineral waters. Dihanesi, it seems, still believes in the efficacy of submerging himself in hot mineral water. He's been staying at the old Brenner's Park Hotel. He takes the waters in his tub, since in the pools he would have to face European women dressed too immodestly for his taste."

"Has anyone important come to see him?" Bolan asked.

"Albrecht Kirchner," Schumann replied with a little smile. "The Knife."

Bolan walked to the riverside and looked back at the slit in the heavy concrete of the old fortification. Two parallel yellow plastic ribbons marked the path of the stream that had been shot from the bunker. Drops of radioactive oil had fallen, and the ground between those two warning ribbons was hot. On the river itself some traffic had resumed. The radioactive slick had moved downstream, and boats chugged around, some of them carrying curiosity seekers who wanted to see the origin of the poisoning.

Schumann raised a pair of small binoculars and scanned the far shore.

"Except for the Iranian—"

Lemaire shook his head at Bolan. "Except for the Iranian, we have no clues," he said. "Well, a small one. An old man who was supposed to guard this place is dead. They killed him. But who? They moved in and out too fast. If we find them, Bolan, we don't argue about the niceties. You understand?''

Bolan nodded. "I understand."

He glanced at Schumann just in time to see the German jerk, clutch his chest and drop to the ground.

A DOZEN HELICOPTERS were flying over the river within minutes, searching for signs of a gunman. But they found nothing. Bolan and Lemaire had dived to the ground and drawn their weapons. Both of them were experienced men who knew what to look for. Neither of them could see where the shot might have come from.

An explosive bullet had torn through Schumann's chest and he'd died almost instantly. His killer, a rifleman, probably firing with a scope, had disappeared.

An hour later, at police headquarters in Strasbourg, Lemaire had been compelled to notify Paris that Heinrich Schumann, agent of the German BND, had been murdered on French soil and that he, Lemaire, had no idea who had done it or where to find the killer.

ILSE VON DER SCHULENBERG, who had slipped back down the bank to her boat and pushed off into the current, had sat in the back and pretended she was having difficulty getting her motor started, until the current swept her past Bolan and Lemaire. Sitting in her small boat, the dark-haired young woman had escaped their attention. She'd been prepared to drop her prized rifle into the river if she had to. She didn't

Half an hour later and five miles downstream, she headed to shore on the German side, went to her car and drove into Baden-Baden. Kirchner was there, and she found him at the Europäischer Hof.

She grinned in triumph. "Bolan is dead." She laughed "Now what?"

9

"Bolan, too," Napoleon Malik said to Hajan Dihanesi.

The Iranian nodded. It was apparent that he didn't think the elimination of the American who was called the Executioner was a matter of any great import. He lifted a cup and sipped the weak, acidic coffee that was all that could be had in most of Europe.

Here, in the privacy of his hotel room in Baden-Baden, he wore the clothing he preferred, a long white robe, a simple black turban.

"So, you see," Malik continued. "With a little restraint, a bit of planning and brilliance in execution, if I may say so, we have won two significant victories."

"But the imperialists show no sign that they are about to make concessions," Dihanesi complained.

"Let them have a few days," Malik suggested. "Then—"

"The Prophet—peace be unto him—does counsel patience," the Iranian agreed, "but let preparations go forward. You have accumulated all your remaining cesium in one place?"

Malik shook his head. "Not in one place, my friend. If we should suffer an attack, we could lose all of it. But all of it is where it can be moved into position in a few hours."

"And this time," Dihanesi said, "they will lose a city?"

"They will lose a city," Malik repeated somberly. "Provided you turn over to us the cesium in your hands."

Dihanesi frowned. "May God forgive us," he said gravely. "For murder is not the way of God."

"He will forgive us."

"If I didn't believe so, I wouldn't take part in this plan," Dihanesi said. "It is only because I believe God wants this work done that I lend my assistance to it. I know no other way that we will wring justice from the imperialist aggressors."

"Then you'll release to us the cesium you're holding?"

Dihanesi nodded. "It will be delivered to you in Beirut. It will double your stock. Use it well."

Malik sighed. "Let's hope we get concessions without having to use it."

The Iranian's chin rose. "Humanity will not be liberated to follow in the ways of God by indulging in hope."

BOLAN SAT in the Frankfurt offices of the Bundesnachtrichtendienst, with Paul Lemaire and a BND section chief named Joseph Dietrich. They were looking at a set of photographs.

"Here is Napoleon Malik," Dietrich said, handing over a picture of a man leaving a hotel. "Do you recognize him, Colonel Pollock?"

"We encountered him in Paris. I didn't get a good look."

"And this is the woman he calls his wife."

Bolan stared thoughtfully at the photograph of the exotically beautiful Jasmin Malik.

"We have these people under surveillance," Dietrich continued. "In truth, you know, we have no grounds to arrest them. Anyway, we think it's better to watch them, to see what they do, who they meet and so on. Do you agree?"

Bolan nodded. "We'll never get to the root of the United Righteous problem just by arresting Malik."

"And here—" the German handed over another photograph "—is a mystery. Who do you suppose she might be?"

The young woman in the picture was quite pretty. The photographs were in color, taken with a high-quality telephoto lens, and her dark eyes and hair, her dark red lipstick and the color of her clothes were all vividly shown. She was wearing loose slacks and a jacket, and her hair was hidden by a scarf.

"A concession to Dihanesi," Dietrich said, putting a finger on the scarf. "He doesn't like to see women's hair."

"I have no idea who she is," Bolan told him.

"Neither have we." Dietrich handed over three more photographs. "Dihanesi's entourage," he said. "Bodyguards, we suppose. Young fellows, hmm? Look at the scar on that one's face. I'm going to make a guess that he got it in the Iran-Iraq war."

"Significant facts," Lemaire said. "All of these people have been across the river. Dihanesi entered France on the very day the radioactive oil was sprayed into the river. He crossed the bridge at Wintersdorf that morning and returned to Germany in the afternoon. The Maliks crossed that bridge the same afternoon, entering Germany."

"The bridge was closed shortly after they crossed," Dietrich said, "because of the radioactivity in the water."

"They had something to do with it," Lemaire stated. "No question. So where do they strike next? For we can't suppose they won't strike again."

"The shot that killed Schumann was meant for me," Bolan stated. "He looked something like me. The rifleman, firing from a distance, took Schumann for me."

"You are in grave danger, my friend," Lemaire said. "We must be on guard."

"SHE'S A BLOODY damned fool," Malik shouted angrily. "Do you know what she's done? She killed an agent of the BND! Not only that. She did it under the very eyes of a high-ranking agent of GIGN, and in his jurisdiction. Do you know what that means? It means that our war has been reduced to a personal vendetta. It was a conflict among professionals, with a little grudging respect accorded on both sides. Now it's a blood feud. Before, you might have been arrested in France and released after a rigorous interrogation. Now, if any one of us is arrested, he will simply disappear. And I could wish that disappear were all of it. No, what will happen will be worse than that. In any case, no trace of us will be found. There will be no record of our painful death."

"You exaggerate," Albrecht Kirchner said uncertainly, not at all sure that Malik did exaggerate.

"Do I?" Malik asked coldly. "GIGN isn't an investigatory agency. It isn't a counterintelligence agency. It's purpose is quite simple—to find the enemies of France and kill them. The West Germans are sensitive about tough police tactics, fearful that another Gestapo should evolve. But when one of their own has been murdered, they'll do exactly what the Gestapo would have done, no less."

"So what do you want to do, kill her?" Kirchner asked, nodding toward Ilse von der Schulenberg who knelt on the floor, her head hung.

"If I thought that dumping her body on the street before GIGN headquarters in Paris would make the least difference, I'd kill her now and dump her," Malik gritted between clenched teeth.

Ilse looked up, unable to conceal her fear, unwilling to conceal her hatred for this man.

"But it wouldn't make any difference," Malik went on. "None at all. They would understand that we had handed them the corpse of the hit man—hit woman—as a peace offering. But they wouldn't make peace. They know very well that one of us, Albrecht—you or I, or Dihanesi or Manero—sent her to kill Bolan. They know that, and they won't be satisfied with the corpse of that bitch. They want *our* corpses now. Ours.''

"I—" Kirchner began.

"Do you understand, Albrecht, that we're not safe? Not in this house, not at this moment. Before, you and I could walk the streets. Dihanesi, he's an Iranian parliamentarian and in a sense untouchable. No more. Because now there will be no arrest. No record. No notice. We will just die. Any one of us.''

"So what do we do?" Kirchner asked.

"Our options have just disappeared," Malik said. "This...*slut* has foreclosed our options. We are hunted men. The force out to kill us is far greater than the force we have sent against Bolan. We have no choice now. We must launch the big operation immediately. If it succeeds, and we gain power, we will survive. If it doesn't, we won't.''

Only when Malik left did Ilse dare rise from her knees. Her legs and back ached. She had knelt—tall, as they put it, with her legs straight and bent only at the knees—for nearly two hours. Malik's woman, Jasmin, had slapped her several times hard across the cheeks, and she hadn't dared protest or resist.

But she had added a new target to her list. She *would* kill Bolan sooner or later. And she would kill Jasmin Malik.

"I will kill Bolan," she promised Kirchner. "I will go to the States tomorrow, at my own expense. I will—"

"No. You'll do as you are told," he said. "You'll go to Beirut with the Maliks. They may need a gun. In any case, they'll need a servant, someone to carry their bags, run their errands. You'll go with them and learn humility and obedience. I'm sure—" he grinned sadistically "—that Jasmin Malik will prove a competent instructor."

SHONDOR SAVACHEVA met Bolan at Kennedy International Airport.

"I've got news," he said.

"I could use some," Bolan replied. "Where are they? What are they doing?"

"Moving, we can be sure of it. They're gone. Disappeared. The Maliks and Kirchner. Hajan Dihanesi has returned to Tehran. No word from them, incidentally. No proclamation. No demands."

Bolan sighed and shook his head. "We've said before, no city is safe."

"We've stepped up security around the major urban reservoirs," Shondor told him. "Troops. National Guard. New York is thought of as specially vulnerable. And, well, of course, the news is full of the poisoning of the Rhine. A lot of people are saying, 'Give these characters what they want. What could they want that's so important?' There are editorials like that. Speeches in Congress.

"The President says it's just like appeasement in the 1930s," he went on. "If we give them what they ask for now, tomorrow they'll want something else. But he's under a lot of pressure to make concessions."

"The people who talk like that don't know what the demands are," Bolan said.

"No. We've never released their proclamations. It's odd that the United Righteous doesn't make them public."

"They know our resistance would stiffen," Bolan replied. "If the English people, for example, had known what Hitler demanded of Chamberlain in 1938, they would never have supported him."

"Well, the President sends a personal message," Shondor said. "'Be careful, Mack. Take care of yourself.' He understands that the shot that killed Heinrich Schumann was meant for you."

"I want to form a small combat force," Bolan said. "I've been thinking of it on the way back across the Atlantic. A few good men with good weapons. If we have to fight the United Righteous again, it won't be as easy as it was in West Virginia."

"I volunteer," Shondor said immediately.

"Thanks. And so will Paul Lemaire. But we'll need some others. I'd guess we only have a few days, maybe a week, to get the force together. Let's give it priority, Shondor. Top priority."

"Suppose we call it Force 90."

IT WASN'T EASY to get into Beirut. The airport was under sporadic attack. Two jetliners had been destroyed by mortar bombs, and nothing was flying. The Maliks and Ilse von der Schulenberg landed at Damascus, unofficial guests of the Syrian government, which neither asked for their passports nor suggested an examination of their luggage.

Ilse was left to retrieve the luggage and carry it to the parking lot, while the Maliks conferred with the Syrian operative who would arrange their transportation to Beirut. Ilse was a servant. If she didn't understand that, Jasmin was there to remind her.

"What you have arranged is very clever, Mr. Malik," said the Syrian operative. "We have done our part, as you suggested."

"I'm grateful."

"The president would like to see you," the Syrian went on. "He realizes, however," the Syrian added smoothly, "that your mission requires close timing and that you must be anxious to move on to Beirut."

In Syria Napoleon Malik was still the respected leader of the Islamic Strike Force, but it was clear that the president didn't want to be identified too closely with the partly discredited leader of the ISF.

"I'm most anxious to move on to Beirut," said Malik, who read both sides of the message.

In other years, other circumstances, the drive from Damascus to Beirut might have required an hour or so. Now the scarred gray Russian-built car, following a military vehicle and trailed by one—all three flying the red-white-black-green Syrian flag—needed almost three hours to make the journey. Twice the little convey left the highway and drove into a dry streambed as roaring jet fighters passed overhead. They were at too high an altitude to be identified, but they could have been Israeli.

The armed driver and guard pointed at the ruins of villages without saying who had destroyed them. Ilse understood they wanted their visitors to think that all the destruction had been caused by Israeli bombers and artillery, but anyone who knew the history of the past few years knew the ruins could have just as likely been caused by fighting among the various Christian and Muslim factions in Lebanon.

As far as Ilse was concerned, it was poor country to be fighting for. Any civilized people, in her judgment, would have said, "Here, take it and be damned. Who wants all this grit and scrub anyway?" It had been ugly *before* it was bombed and shelled, she thought. Who could love it?

The Maliks, she could tell, were moved by what they saw. She wasn't sure what kind of Arab Napoleon Malik was, but he might well be on his home ground.

As they approached Beirut they were stopped repeatedly. It seemed everyone had roadblocks. Usually it was impossible to tell what faction had stopped the vehicle. It made no difference; they had the guns to make you stop. The Syrian flags counted for something, but not enough to make these armed boys stand aside.

Boys. Never in her life had she seen such fierce hatred. Their eyes burned with it, obsessed, fanatic hatred, as a way of life, without their even knowing for sure who they hated or why. It was apparent in their eyes, all over their faces, even in the way they carried their bodies. Hatred, yes, but coupled with dismal hopelessness, despair, frustration. The zealots of Baader-Meinhof or the Red Brigades had hated, but never like this. They had always known who they hated and why; but if she understood these children, *they* didn't know.

She sensed that the Maliks were uneasy. No—they were afraid.

Beirut burned. Black smoke hung over the city. Ilse was surprised that anything remained to burn. But this afternoon, as the driver explained, rockets from somewhere to the south had poured into the city, indiscriminately demolishing homes, stores, schools and setting fires that couldn't be put out until the gunmen in the streets would let the fire brigades through.

Who had fired these rockets?

Israelis, he said—though obviously that wasn't true.

How Dihanesi could have found a pleasant small house facing the sea in this besieged city, it was difficult to say. But he had. The Syrian military cars fell away a mile or so from the Dihanesi villa, and the driver got out and took the Syrian flags off the fenders of the car. A few minutes later the gray car pulled into a tiny, palm-shaded courtyard before a modest stucco house, and the Iranian himself opened the door and spread his arms in a gesture of welcome.

More at his ease in a country at least partly Islamic, he stood in the doorway in a robe of white with violet pin-stripes, with a thin white turban wrapped around his head.

He welcomed Malik, and he nodded at Jasmin. He glanced scornfully at Ilse and said, "Cover her head and her legs before she enters my house."

IN A DOZEN thick lead boxes in the cellar under the house, 18 pounds of cesium 137 lay in sealed platinum capsules. It was fifty times the amount introduced into the swimming pools on Majorca, a hundred times the amount that caused the disaster in Goiânia.

"I understand the cesium is very beautiful," Dihanesi said. "That it glows with an unearthly blue light."

Malik nodded. "I understand that is so. And those who see that light die."

"How are you going to ship it?"

Malik smiled. "Quite simply, actually. Inside computers."

"Computers?"

"Yes. An American company has twenty small computers in Riyadh, where they have been demonstrating some marvelous technology to the Saudis. Those are going back to America soon. Each one will have inside a small lead capsule, and inside the lead capsule will be a platinum capsule. You see?"

"There is space?"

"Each little computer contains what the Americans call a 'mother board.' If you remove it—that is, remove it without knowing precisely what you are doing—you can destroy the board and the computer. So customs inspectors look at these expensive little machines, understand that only a tiny quantity of heroin or cocaine could be concealed inside them—for which it is not worth destroying them—and pass them through. Each one can carry enough cesium to kill ten thousand people."

Dihanesi smiled. "And those computers aren't something being imported into the United States. They are something going back."

"Exactly."

"And do the Saudis know?"

Malik laughed. "Do those aristocrats know anything? Those desert noblemen? They wouldn't know how to scratch their balls without Americans or Europeans to teach them how."

"Ah..." Dihanesi chuckled. "The custodians of the holy places. One day—"

"One day," Malik said, "the places touched by the Prophet's foot will abide in holier hands."

For a moment Dihanesi stared quizzically at Malik. Then he grinned and laughed. "Not your hands, friend."

Malik shook his head. "Of course not. What would I do with the holy places? Better in *your* hands, Hojatolislam."

Dihanesi's face turned abruptly solemn. "In the name of God may it be so. May every unholy alliance be terminated, and may the faithful own the holy places."

AN HOUR LATER he grinned at Malik and asked, "Can your women entertain?"

"Of course. What entertainment do you have in mind?"

"Ah, dancers. With their hair uncovered—and other parts. Entertainment such as women owe men."

"Dancers," Malik mused. "Well, why not?"

A little later he told Jasmin and Ilse what was demanded. "A bit of dancing to music from the radio while we eat. It's what the man expects. It's an easy way to amuse him, keep the peace with him."

The two women did as they were asked. They danced for the men at dinner, for Dihanesi and Malik, and for the Syrian driver and guard who had brought them to Beirut, also for two of Dihanesi's bodyguards. Neither of them had any skill at Oriental dancing. Neither had a costume. In their lingerie they went woodenly through the motions of a belly dance, to the rhythm of Arab music from a small radio. For them the performance was an awkward, degrading spectacle. The men were amused.

"I believe I will be entertained privately by that one," Dihanesi said quietly to Malik, pointing to Jasmin. "That is, if you have no objections. I know she is spoken of as your wife, but I understand she is rather your servant."

Malik nodded. "She is my servant, and you are welcome to enjoy her."

Without a word of objection, Jasmin went to a second-floor bedchamber and waited for the Iranian. In half an hour he arrived.

She was ready, naked as he would expect.

Hajan Dihanesi got undressed and lay down.

"You have been punished for your crimes against God," he said, running a finger down across the scars on her back.

"My crimes against man," she replied bitterly.

"Against God," he repeated firmly. "The Prophet gave man the laws of God. You were treated leniently. If I had been your judge—"

Dihanesi wasn't able to finish the sentence. She drove a long, thin knife between his ribs—once, twice, a third time. As he choked on the blood rising in his throat, his eyes widened, and he stared at her face in disbelief.

She smiled. "Good night, mullah."

JASMIN SHOOK MALIK AWAKE.

"The Iranian is dead. We must be on our way before his body is discovered."

Malik jerked upright. "You—"

"It's what he deserved," she replied crisply.

Malik scrambled out of bed. Ilse was there with him—which Jasmin chose to ignore after a short contemptuous glance—and he wakened her.

"I have taken care of one of his bodyguards," Jasmin said coldly. "Is either of you capable of doing the others?"

Ilse rolled off her side of the bed, already alert, and began to pull on her clothes. "All right," she said. "The crap is over. Give me a gun."

Malik pulled a valise toward him, opened it and handed her a silenced Taurus automatic. The Taurus was a Brazilian duplicate of the Beretta 92, a 9 mm weapon with all the power and reliability of the pistol on which it was modeled.

Ilse pulled the slide on the Taurus to be sure there was a round in the chamber, and shoved the round she had ejected into the breast pocket of her blouse. She favored each of the Maliks with a glance of utter contempt and stalked out of the room.

Within half a minute they heard the muffled pop of the first shot fired from the silenced pistol. Then they heard the second.

Ilse returned. "You screwed up," she said to them. She scowled at Jasmin. "You, especially, bitch. Get the goddam bags together. I'll roust out the chauffeur."

THE DEMONSTRATION computers were shipped from Riyadh the following Monday. Ilse, her American passport bearing the name Madeleine Dallas, arrived on the same flight and accepted them at Kennedy International as the representative of TT&D—Texas Telecommunications and Digital. The capsules of cesium 137 went undetected.

So did her target rifle, also disassembled and packed inside the housings of two of the computers.

"WE DON'T KNOW the objective," a grimfaced Mack Bolan said to the assembled men. "We don't know where they'll strike. That's why I've chosen personnel with various language skills. Commands have to be issued in one common language, which will be English. From this moment on, the use of any other language, even in personal conversation, is out. Understood?"

"Ich verstehe, Herr Oberst." One of the men laughed. He was Karl Oberfallen, an agent of BND detached and assigned to Force 90.

"Oui, mon Colonel," Paul Lemaire answered, taking up the joke.

"Capisco," Tony Balducci added.

Bolan laughed, the tension effectively relieved. To Oberfallen and Balducci he was Colonel Rance Pollack. Only Lemaire and Shondor Savacheva knew him as Bolan.

"We're informal," the warrior went on. "We have no sanction from any government. Our purpose is to prevent a disaster any way we have to do it, no matter what. We'll have covert support from the government of any country where we work, and when we work inside a country we'll probably be joined by new, local recruits. What we do is absolutely secret. Part of our job is to prevent panic. I hope we can do what we have to do without anybody knowing it."

They met in a small lodge on a New England lake, in the middle of what was a boys' summer camp. The first snow had fallen and a thin layer of ice covered the lake.

Bolan looked at the men and shook his head. "Some of you need physical training but there isn't time for it. We have to depend on what you can do, as you are. Most of you, though, will find our weapons new. I respect your personal choices. I respect, Paul, your MAT 49. The French manufacture good weapons. We'll use American weapons mostly, not because they're necessarily better, but because we need to standardize."

"Standardize on the best, then," Oberfallen suggested.

"Right," said Bolan. "I shouldn't have said American. I should have said weapons that Americans recognize, respect and have adopted. Our assault rifle is of German manufacture. Some of our pistols are Italian. I ask every one of you to become one-hundred-percent familiar with and proficient with the weapons I've chosen."

He lifted from the table a Heckler & Koch G-11 caseless assault rifle.

"Some of you haven't fired one of these before," he said. "It's new. There are no cartridges, no brass casings for gunpowder. When you fire a round, the propellant sends the bullet out of the barrel and so doing burns up, disappears. There's no empty shell casing to be ejected. That means the next round goes immediately into the chamber, ready to fire, which means this rifle can fire two thousand rounds a minute."

"It's plastic," Lemaire said, a little scornfully.

"Some," Bolan agreed. "It won't rust. It takes shock, dirt, water... you name it. It has an optical sight—molded in, so it can't be knocked off target. I've used this weapon, and it fires smoothly and accurately. It'll hit what you aim at, and its penetrating power is formidable. I'd appreciate it if in the next twenty-four hours each of you would put two or three thousand rounds through the one that's handed to you. When you've done that, you'll have as much confidence in it as I have—and that's essential."

Lemaire walked to the table and picked up a G-11, hefted it skeptically, peered through the sight and shrugged.

"When we operate as a unit," Bolan said, "we'll have with us an XM-174 automatic grenade launcher." He stepped to the end of the table, where the odd-looking machine stood on its tripod. "I want each of you to learn to operate this. It can get rid of twelve grenades in three or four seconds, and, believe me, the people on the other end will know they're under fire. In a pinch you can fire it from the hip."

He picked it up to show them that the weapon wasn't heavy—less than twenty-five pounds with a magazine of twelve grenades mounted.

"These are weapons of war," Lemaire observed.

Bolan nodded. "Any of you think what we're up against is anything less?"

NAPOLEON MALIK and Albrecht Kirchner sat together in a flat overlooking the Champs Elysées in Paris, reading a printed paper.

Death Sentence

The satanic demons Napoleon Malik and Albrecht Kirchner, together with their whores Ilse von der Schulenberg and Aisha Nusrat, the already-condemned criminal who escaped most of her punishment, are condemned to death for their monstrous crime of murder against the virtuous and holy man, the Hojatolislam Hajan Dihanesi! This sentence is imposed by the new governing council of the Islamic Strike Force!

"Ten thousand copies," Malik said. "A hundred thousand. Who knows?"

"Your woman—"

"And yours. If we could offer them in requital..."

"Gladly," Kirchner agreed.

Malik shook his head sadly. "Under the law, they are *ours*. We're responsible for what they do."

"Then?"

"Then," Malik replied, "we have one choice and one choice only. We must bring down the imperialist democracies. We—"

"Talk sense," Kirchner spit contemptuously.

"If," Malik said, "we destroy a major city, the western nations will surrender to us. What else can they do? What would they bomb to stop us? Tehran? Damascus? They'll have to deal with us. And when they do, we will have *power*. Then...then, my friend, the new governing council of the Islamic Strike Force will have to deal with us, too."

"We collect our loyalists..."

"Yes," Malik said. "A few good men. That's the key, always—a few good men. Give me ten good men rather than a thousand believers. They're all we need."

"The two women?" Kirchner asked.

Malik grinned. "I *bought* mine. How did you get yours? She has become an inconvenience. I'll rid myself of her. And you?"

"Yes. Ilse von der Schulenberg has made too many errors."

Napoleon Malik stood at the window, parted the curtains and looked down on the evening traffic in Paris. This city was beautiful, endlessly beautiful, but he was here now only because the French didn't know where he was. When he was victorious in his war against the... Against who, really? Against those who resisted him, whoever, for whatever reason. When he had won his war, he would live here in Paris in a larger and more luxurious flat than this—as a master, as a guest the French would be glad to have within their borders.

Kirchner poured generous drinks of old brandy into two snifters and handed one to Malik.

"To success," Kirchner said.

"Yes. Over *all* our enemies."

"So, on to Los Angeles!"

"On to Los Angeles!"

10

Force 90 was easily trained. Men like Shondor Savacheva, Paul Lemaire, Karl Oberfallen and Tony Balducci had little to learn about the war between civilization and barbarism. Each one, in his own way, had done his work and suffered the scars.

Oberfallen, whose grandfather has served in Hitler's SS, was credited with the elimination of the neo-Nazi organization called the Black Flag. Tony Balducci had rid Italy of a prominent cell of Red Brigades. Both men had used tactics the Executioner had used many times over. Their governments pretended not to know them.

All these men took their new weapons with professional insight. Within half an hour of being introduced to them, they were chopping up targets with accurate fire or blowing them to bits with well-directed grenades. These were the men who knew how to appreciate the tools of combat.

Each man kept his personal side arm. Bolan would use the .44 Magnum Desert Eagle. Shondor and Balducci would use the Beretta 92. Lemaire didn't carry a pistol, insisting that a mini-Uzi didn't impede his movements and suited him best. Oberfallen, strangely, elected to carry a 9 mm Luger. It had been his grandfather's.

The problem now was the waiting.

The force—except for Bolan and Shondor Savacheva—stayed at the camp on the lake, where the snow fell every day and grew deeper, and the lake froze. A fast military helicopter stood ready to take them out any time. They played cards, took more practice with their weapons and, as Paul insisted, ate and drank well while they waited for the call.

The helicopter would deliver them to Otis Air Force Base, from which a small, fast jet would take them anywhere in the world within a few hours.

But where?

THE MEN WERE EASY enough to please, and a girl could be totally inconspicuous pleasing them—inconspicuous to the point of disappearing. Ilse was working as a topless dancer on a square little stage in the middle of a bar on La Cienega Boulevard, where men came to drink and stare—hardhats, tourists, students from Southern Cal. It was funny, really, how being on display made her inconspicuous.

It was funny how they thought she should be embarrassed. In fact, they wouldn't have enjoyed her little performance if they hadn't supposed she did it only reluctantly and because she desperately needed the money.

She had taken the little computers to the supposed site of Texas Telecommunications and Digital in Austin, and in a motel room there she had disassembled them one by one and removed the platinum-and-lead capsules containing the cesium 137.

But not before she bought a Geiger counter. Trust Albrecht Kirchner and Napoleon Malik? Only a fool would have trusted them. She recovered the computers at the intercontinental airport in Houston, after U.S. customs agents cleared them, and flew them on a local flight to Austin. She let them sit in a warehouse on the airport until she got her own radiation counter, and only when she could check for herself did she begin to disassemble the desktop computers and remove the capsules.

The capsules were safe. Each one contained enough deadly radioactive cesium to kill a thousand people, but the lead and platinum contained the radiation. She carried them to California in nothing more dramatic than a nylon beach bag.

She rented a car and drove to Los Angeles, amazed, as she had often been before, at the way Americans crossed their state borders and no one ever asked anybody what they were carrying.

Another interesting thing about the United States was the ease with which she bought a weapon. In a shop in Arizona she pretended she knew little or nothing about handguns but felt a need to protect herself. The man behind the counter sold her what he called a S&W Model 19, a snub-nosed revolver that fired .357 Magnum ammunition. He even took her into a pistol range behind the store and let her fire it—while he fondled her breasts as she pretended to learn how to handle the heavy handgun.

Americans—they loved to look at breasts, loved to pet them. When she suggested she didn't want to be registered as a purchaser, the man shoved his hand up under her shirt, had a good feel and let her walk out the door with an unregistered revolver.

Each night she danced on the little stage, bare-breasted, and waited for a contact.

THE MALIKS ARRIVED in the United States separately, he through Boston in the persona of a Lebanese businessman come to arrange the importation of Lebanese wines, she through Los Angeles, traveling as the wife of a Chilean who was already in the States as a broker in Chilean agricultural products.

Albrecht Kirchner arrived at Kennedy International on the day Jasmin Malik landed in Los Angeles. He came as a buyer, hoping to find an American company willing to sell him certain chemicals essential to a sophisticated color-photography process.

They had agreed not to meet, not even to contact one another, until everything was in order for the attack on the Los Angeles water supply. Each one had an assignment—as Ilse had been assigned to accompany the cesium into Houston and move it to California.

Napoleon Malik was to assemble a team from the few members of the Islamic Strike Force who were in the United States. There were only eight of them, five enrolled as students at American universities. All were young men utterly dedicated to the destruction of the world's imperialist aggressors. If anything, Malik knew, they could be a little *too* dedicated.

As a European, Kirchner was best able to disappear in the United States. Within an hour after he passed through Kennedy, he was on his way to California, driving a car that wasn't rented but was ostensibly his, titled in the name of his driver's license—Fred Wilkinson, of Cleveland, Ohio. In California he'd contact two friends of the late Isoroku Akada, members of Red Nippon. Together they would handle the logistics of the operation. He had carried no weapons into the States. Obtaining the right weapons was essential.

Jasmin Malik was to kill Bolan. If she could find him.

Ilse had no assignment to kill Bolan, but she was determined to do it, if she could find any way to get him in the sights of her rifle.

"I'VE GOT a very odd request," the President of the United States said to Hal Brognola. "It may be a trap to get Bolan in a position to be killed or a ruse to get him and his team away from where the real action is going to happen."

"For the latter to be the case, sir, they'd have to know about Force 90," Brognola suggested. "We've kept the secret pretty well, I think."

"Actually," the President said, "they don't even ask for Bolan. Not by name, anyway. I should let you read the message. It's from the president of Iraq, and I don't suppose I need to tell you how very confidential it is. He's asking for help."

"An odd source for a request for American help," Brognola replied.

The President nodded his agreement as he passed the message across the desk.

To the President of the United States of America from the President of the Republic of Iraq, Greeting in the name of God, and benevolent good wishes.

We have learned, of recent date, that a large quantity of poisonous radioactive material, stolen from other countries we have no doubt, since our own nation produces no such material, has been secreted in caves in one of our most remote regions. Conscious of the responsibility of civilized nations to identify such materials and make their existence known to the international community that a repetition of the catastrophic poisonings of Majorca and of the Rhine may be avoided, we have sought to discover the specific location of these materials that we might place them under lawful guard and prevent their misuse.

Unhappily we find—and in this we speak in complete confidence—that a handful of our military officers are not to be trusted in this regard. It is our wish to mount an effective operation to discover these materials, to overcome such forces as may be guarding them and to bring them within our control.

In this respect, it is our understanding that you maintain a small force capable of quick entry and exit, which might have the ability to make a rapid and secret strike on this probable cache of radioactive poisons. If this is true and if you are so inclined, we would be pleased to enter into confidential discussions immediately, looking to the temporary presence within our borders of such a force and looking also to a cooperative effort to achieve what must be a mutual purpose.

Can we in any way lay greater emphasis on the necessity of your treating this communication as a state secret and the further necessity of our discussions and any subsequent operations remaining permanently confidential?

I await your reply.

"The Joint Chiefs say no," the President said. "They say he wants to get those materials in his hands so he can use them his own way. In fact the CIA says the Iraqi government has been stockpiling bomb-quality material in these caves for some time. The CIA says the Islamic Strike Force carried out some raids on the trucks carrying the material which is where what was sprayed into the Rhine may have come from. The CIA thinks the president's real problem is that the ISF has now simply seized the caves and is holding his radioactive material, and that he doesn't dare go in with a force to take it back because many of his officers are more sympathetic to the ISF than they are to him. Anyway, the Joint Chiefs say what the president of Iraq may want to do with that material is as much to be feared as what the ISF may want to do with it."

Brognola shook his head. "If he misused the stuff in any way—or even showed signs of intention to do so—we could publish his communication," he said. "His government wouldn't last a day after that."

"I agree. Do you really suppose the big stockpile is in caves in Iraq? Or—"

"Or are we being suckered," Brognola finished the sentence.

"Right. Which?"

"Bolan's team is trained and ready," the big Fed replied. "And right now it's doing nothing."

"That's not good for a combat force."

"No. On the other hand, we can't spare them very long. Say thirty-six hours, in and out. And that's what the president wants—in and out fast. What's more, it gives us a chance to destroy the stockpile, if that's what's there. Secretly. No questions asked."

"You'd go for it," the President said.

"If Bolan will. We can't give him orders."

THERE WAS LITTLE time to plan. Too little. Bolan liked improvised operations and was good at them, but this one was a little *too* informal.

The Iraqis had supplied aerial recon photos of the cave area and had said they would supply a guide. Otherwise they were staying out of it.

There were a thousand ways this operation could go wrong, and just one way it could go right—which was that it could eliminate a stockpile of radioactive material that had been accumulated for no possible good reason.

One more man was added to Force 90—David Syrkin, the Mossad agent who had been with the Executioner in the street fight in Paris. Since David spoke a little Arabic, he might prove to be a useful man on this mission.

The president of Iraq had been told only that a force would arrive by air. He wasn't told where it was coming

from, and he didn't ask. Maybe he suspected the American
force would fly from Israel, which was exactly where it did
fly from. David Syrkin joined Force 90 at the airport at
Haifa.

The aircraft was a Hercules C-130, a lot of airplane for a
force of only six men, but it carried two armored scout cars
as well as the men and their equipment, plus a crew of four.
Besides, for this flight an aircraft with substantial range was
necessary. It was like all C-130s, a fat fuselage, high wings,
four turboprop engines, an auxiliary fuel tank slung under
the wings between each pair of engines. A workhorse airplane, it was capable of landing on small airports, even on
grass strips.

The Hercules took off from Haifa an hour after midnight. It flew west briefly, then turned north and flew parallel to the coastline of Lebanon and Syria, about fifty miles
out. After a little less than an hour, the aircraft crossed the
coast of Turkey and turned east. The Turks had consented
to this flight over their airspace, requiring from the government of the United States only a vague assurance that the
flight represented an extremely important mission and was
nonaggressive.

Another hour brought the flight to the Iraqi border, where
the Hercules turned south. A short while later it landed at
the airport in the city of Mosul.

The airport was in complete darkness, all but abandoned. The arrival of an American aircraft was expected,
and security forces had been pulled back. The Hercules,
expertly handled by experienced Air Force pilots, touched
down not far from the threshold of the runway and came to
a quick stop about two-thirds of the way along its length.

The crew included two Air Force sergeants, cargo han-
dlers, who let down the rear ramp almost before the Hercules came to a stop. Bolan and Shondor Savacheva were

first out of the plane, carrying their G-11 assault rifles. Within a minute the two armored scout cars had been driven down the ramp and were on the runway. The rest of the force climbed into the vehicles.

Bolan trotted back inside the airplane for a final word with the pilots.

"Twenty-two hundred hours, right?"

"You got it, Colonel."

"Watch for the flares. If anything's wrong, we'll do our best to warn you off."

"Good luck, sir."

As soon as the warrior was out again, the ramp was retracted and the rear doors closed. Then, having reversed the pitch on his propellers, the pilot backed the Hercules along the runway to the spot where he had touched down. He didn't have to turn off onto a taxiway. He could simply back up. A minute and a half later the big transport rushed along the runway and lifted off, climbing steeply away into the darkness.

"Colonel Pollock," David Syrkin began. "Our host . . ."

While Bolan had been talking to the pilot, then watching the takeoff, an Iraqi officer had arrived in a small car and had engaged in conversation with the only man who could fully understand his language.

"He says he knows who we are and why we're here. He says he has cleared the way for us, through the routine road checks along the airport road. He also says he's brought us a guide, which is a problem. The guide speaks Kurdish."

"And none of us does."

"Even our host," Syrkin replied. "He tells me it will make no difference. Even if we can't talk, the man will show us where to go."

Bolan shrugged. "We'll have to make do."

He turned and looked at the man. The guide was in early middle age, his skin leathery from exposure to sun and wind. He wore a pair of loose pants, tattered and stained, an oversized shirt, a turban wrapped around his head and sandals. He carried a Kalashnikov AK-47 assault rifle.

"The officer says the man's name is Ali Ibrahim. He's a shepherd. He has seen them carrying radioactive materials into the caves."

Bolan shook hands with the guide, then climbed aboard one of the armored scout vehicles with him.

The two scout cars were of French manufacture. They had been chosen for the mission because cars of that type had been exported from France to every nation in the Middle East over the years, and if two of them, unmarked, were found in Iraq, they wouldn't announce that an American military force had been in the country. In any case, Bolan knew them to be reliable vehicles.

The car was manufactured by a company called Panhard and was known as AML, which when translated, meant a light scout car. It was a four-wheeled vehicle sitting high on big tires, its engine in the rear. Different versions of the AML were variously armed. The two belonging to the team were equipped with twin 7.62 mm machine guns set in small rotating turrets, and each also carried a 60 mm mortar. The driver rode inside the armored body, with his head protruding through a hatch. Two crewmen rode in the broad open hatch on top of the turret. Two or three infantrymen could ride on the rear deck above the engine.

Bolan rode in the turret on the first car, with the guide beside him. Syrkin was the driver. Oberfallen rode behind the turret. Balducci drove the second car, with Shondor and Lemaire in the turret.

Syrkin had tried his Arabic on the guide. Ibrahim understood a word or two maybe, but clearly he spoke Kurdish and supposed that any civilized man in the world did, too. As they drove out of the airport, Bolan studied a map and gave directions to the Israeli. Ibrahim was puzzled, apparently, at how a man could find his way anywhere by staring at a sheet of paper. The officer had warned that this guide would be useless until they were within a few miles of land he knew.

They had roughly a hundred miles to drive and with luck would reach the hills and caves about dawn.

Mosul was in the valley of the Tigris River. The ancient city of Nineveh was on the other side of the river. Armies had fought over this land two thousand years before Christ. It had been rough, arid land then—except in the valley of the great river—and it was rough, arid land now, occupied by poor farmers and the herders of sheep and goats for centuries. Once they were a little distance from the airport, hardly anyone noticed the two military vehicles passing by in the night. They were nothing unusual.

Now and again Ibrahim would nudge Bolan with an elbow, point to something and speak a few words. He seemed to suppose Bolan would understand what he said. As they covered miles, Ibrahim's nudges and words became more frequent. Bolan understood that the man had begun to see landmarks that he knew and was explaining.

The eastern sky began to lighten; the sun would rise in an hour.

All of them were dressed for combat, even Paul Lemaire who was a policeman and in no sense a soldier. Bolan had suggested he stay behind, but the Frenchman had refused emphatically, saying he had joined this group for better or for worse, and if worse had come to an expedition in the Iraqi desert then he would go with the others.

As they progressed through the desert, hills on both sides of the road rose higher with each passing mile. As the sky reddened and light came to the hillsides, Bolan could see sparse vegetation growing on the higher ground. The guide pointed to a shepherd attending a flock on one of the slopes.

Now at a crossroads Ali Ibrahim pointed firmly to the right. Bolan tapped Syrkin on the head and pointed right. The driver turned the scout car onto a narrower, rough road.

Two miles down the rutted track they came across an abandoned truck, sitting to one side of the road—a wheel was blown off and bullet holes pocked the cab and body. The guide explained what had happened—in Kurdish.

Bolan began to wonder if the man would guide them straight into destruction. Then he saw Ali Ibrahim check his Kalashnikov and begin to scan the hillsides with a newly sharpened eye. Syrkin noticed and slowed down.

Ibrahim touched Syrkin on the head as he had seen Bolan do and made an unmistakable gesture to stop.

Then he pointed at the two scout cars and put his hands on his ears—they made too much noise. The drivers understood and shut off the engines.

Ali Ibrahim pointed up the hillside and set off climbing.

"The two drivers and Lemaire stay with the cars," Bolan ordered. "Inside. Be ready with those twin 7.62s. Oberfallen and Shondor come with me."

He trotted up the hillside after the guide. Wearing nothing on his feet but simple sandals, the guide climbed over rocks and prickly vegetation that clung to the ground. He reached the top of a ridge and turned to wait for Bolan and the others. When the Executioner was beside him, the Iraqi squatted on the ground and pointed.

Bolan saw what he meant. From his height they could see the caves where the radioactive material was supposed to be, and the warrior could see and understand the lay of the land.

The ridge was the first of a series that rose higher and higher to the west. Above and behind them the ridges were green—nothing that could be called pastures, but green enough apparently to support the small herds of sheep and goats that grazed up there. The road followed the turns in a narrow valley. Other ridges, other grazing land, rose on the other side.

Bolan could see the two scout cars below. A few hundred yards farther, the road turned sharply to the north, and a little after that it followed the valley east. In the second turn an almost invisible track ran into a shallower small valley. That track led to a sort of camp, a couple of small wooden buildings, some tents and half a dozen parked trucks. A hill rose sharply behind, and he had to suppose that among the rocks beyond the camp lay the openings into the caves.

This was what he was supposed to attack. It was unfortunate that his intel was so incomplete. He needed to be more certain that he wasn't about to assault a mining camp.

On the other hand, Brognola had assured him that word had come from the President. . . .

Shondor caught up. He and Oberfallen had been slowed down a little by the weight of the MX-174 grenade launcher and magazines of grenade cartridges.

"There it is," Bolan said quietly, pointing to the rude camp.

Shondor raised his binoculars, and surveyed the area. He had been suspicious from the beginning that the whole operation might be a trap, so he took his time and scanned the ridges and valley.

"Did anybody tell you we'd be attacking an army?" he asked Bolan. He handed over the binoculars. "Take a look."

There were two ordinary American pickups, battered and dusty, and a bigger truck, a Mercedes. Three others were small military vehicles, lightly armored, with canvas-covered beds. Each one was mounted with a machine gun. On the ground in the middle of the parked trucks Bolan could see two mortars—and maybe there were more.

"They're not awake yet," Bolan grunted.

"But the sun's going to come up behind them," Shondor said. "If we try to take them from here, we've got to attack before sunrise."

Bolan shook his head. "If we go around and get up behind them, they're going to be awake and moving." He scanned the terrain behind the camp. "Besides, from up here we have a good field of fire. From behind them, we'd have trouble covering the whole area."

Shondor glanced all around one more time, then shrugged. "You're the guy who knows how to do it."

The Executioner had made up his mind. "Keep an eye out. I'm going down to talk with the rest of the team."

He trotted back down the long rough slope. In a minute or so he had explained the situation and given orders to Syrkin, Balducci and Lemaire. Then he made his way back to the crest of the ridge.

"Okay, we move," he said. He patted the fat barrel of the grenade launcher. "This is going to be the difference."

Bolan set off along the ridge toward the northeast, intending to launch his attack from directly above the camp and the mouths of the caves. Shondor and Oberfallen followed, Shondor carrying the XM-174, which weighed about sixteen pounds, plus two 12-round magazines of 40 mm grenade cartridges. Oberfallen carried four more magazines.

Ali Ibrahim brought up the rear, looking highly skeptical.

In five minutes the group was in position about five hundred yards from the camp, which was beyond the range of the grenade launcher. They paused while Bolan surveyed the camp again through Shondor's binoculars.

Two men in ragged blue jeans and OD fatigue jackets were up and moving around. Each carried an assault rifle slung over his shoulder, a Kalashnikov. The Soviets and their satellites had exported these deadly weapons everywhere. Terrorists prized them. But they were standard issue for the Red Army, too, and tens of thousands of the weapons had been captured in Afghanistan.

The force moved in response to Bolan's signals. No more voice commands. He gestured for a slow, quiet move down the slope.

Ali Ibrahim moved up beside the warrior and took the lead, scanning the ground ahead and pointing silently to loose rocks they should avoid, bushes that would rustle or crack if stepped on, and even a deadly viper that slithered away. Bolan touched the Iraqi's shoulder and pointed back. The man had guided them. He wasn't part of the attack.

But Ibrahim grinned and stroked the stock of his weapon. He pointed down toward the camp and set off again.

As they descended, the shadows deepened. The sun was behind the hill opposite, and it was glaring hard on the higher ridges. The contrast between the brightness above and the shadows below was an advantage Bolan understood and appreciated.

Ali Ibrahim scurried forward, agile and amazingly quiet. Finally Bolan had to stop. When the man looked around, the warrior had to signal him to return. Shondor and Oberfallen had caught up now, and Bolan pointed at the XM-174. By gesture he tried to convey the idea that they were now in range. The Iraqi seemed to understand. He stepped aside and watched curiously as Bolan and Shondor set up the grenade launcher.

The XM-174 resembled a machine gun, but it was boxy and the barrel was a tube. On the rear was a pistol grip and trigger. The mount, which was splayfooted and gave it a secure base, was adjustable for windage and elevation.

Bolan sat down on the ground behind the launcher and selected a cartridge. He'd brought rounds that would spray steel pellets, mostly, but he also had one magazine of white phosphorus.

He mounted a magazine of high-explosive, pellet-hurling rounds. The magazine was a sort of oversized can, and with it in place the XM-174 looked awkward and unbalanced.

Not to worry. He estimated the range at two hundred and fifty yards, adjusted the sight and was ready.

When Bolan pulled the trigger, a grenade cartridge flew from the tube, arced over the remaining yards of the slope and fell near one of the pickup trucks. It exploded with a fierce, authoritative blast and peppered the truck with pellets that blew tires, shattered glass and penetrated fenders and doors.

Men immediately swarmed into the area, some piling out of the trucks, others climbing from behind rocks, some rushing out of the shacks and tents. All were armed, and they began to fire indiscriminately, not yet knowing where to aim.

Bolan adjusted his elevation. The first shot had fallen a little short. Now he raised the barrel of the XM-174 a little and pulled the trigger again.

This grenade fell among the wildly firing gunmen, its burst of furious power taking out at least three.

This was the right range. The XM-174 could fire on full automatic, loosing the remaining ten grenade cartridges in this magazine in five seconds; but Bolan chose to be more selective with his fire. He squeezed the trigger three times, sending three more cartridges flying into the midst of the milling gunmen.

The camp was in chaos, but most of the gunmen below were disciplined and, from the look of what they did, were combat-experienced. In the midst of the terror of the barrage of grenades, some of them acted like soldiers. Within a minute, many were down and shielding themselves in or behind the bodies of the vehicles in their camp. Some began to return fire.

They couldn't see where the grenades were coming from, exactly, but they had to be coming from a limited area. Two men had climbed up onto trucks and begun to fire the mounted machine guns, sweeping the slope. They were wide of the mark, but if they kept it up, sooner or later a stream of fire would find Bolan's group.

The distinctive harsh noise of an automatic assault rifle all but deafened Bolan. He turned to see what was going on and saw Ali Ibrahim, prone and aiming a burst toward one of the machine gunners. His first burst was wide. His second missed the gunner but ripped into the truck. The gunner jumped into the bed of the vehicle and left his machine gun silent.

Shondor and Oberfallen joined in. Their G-11s were capable of sending deadly streams of slugs into the camp, and in seconds they were prone and firing.

Bolan moved the launcher's barrel a little to the right and loosed three more grenades. Then he moved to the left of center and fired three more.

The six grenades detonated, but found no victims. The gunmen knew what they faced now, and had found cover. But the grenades served a purpose. The gunmen were off balance and unable to coordinate a counterattack.

A minute later a mortar bomb fell fifty yards behind Bolan and blew a hole in the hard, rocky ground. Earth and stone flew into the air, then fell to the ground in a pelting rain.

"Big son of a bitch," Oberfallen observed, meaning that the mortar had dropped a heavy round. A direct hit wasn't necessary. Close would be good enough.

Bolan grabbed another magazine and this time set the launcher on full automatic. Twelve grenades flew into the middle of the parked trucks and the explosions, coming so rapidly on top of one another shocked the enemy. For a long moment their guns were silenced.

But they were soldiers and assessed the effect of heavy fire—that it caused casualties but didn't leave them unable to defend themselves. Within a minute, two more big mortar rounds fell on the hill, once again wide of Bolan and his men but fearfully destructive and filled with the threat of what would happen if they fell closer.

The Executioner reached for the magazine of phosphorus rounds and jammed it in place on the XM-174. Before he fired, he pulled the signal pistol from his kit and fired a red flare high into the sky. Then in three quick bursts he sent a dozen white phosphorus grenades into the enemy camp.

The grenades burst, hurling white-hot flaming phosphorus and filling the area with choking smoke.

Bolan snatched the XM-174 from its tripod, shoved a magazine of regular grenades into place and stalked down the slope, firing the launcher from the hip.

Shondor and Oberfallen walked abreast, also firing from the hip, sending vicious bursts of fire into the enemy compound. Ali Ibrahim strode alongside. Careful of his ammunition, he stopped every few steps to fire a selective round or two.

Bolan fired a grenade every few seconds, enough to keep the gunmen below off balance.

It was then that the hardmen realized they were fighting only four men. But suddenly two armored scout cars roared up the track, turrets swinging from side to side, the muzzle flames from twin machine guns sweeping back and forth.

That was the final straw—incessant grenades, accurate fire from sharpshooters and now a hurricane of machine-gun fire from two rapidly advancing armored cars. The hardmen cut and ran.

BOLAN FOUND exactly what Hal Brognola had said he would find—an extensive cache of deadly radioactive material stored in drums in four caves. He'd brought a Geiger counter and discovered that the mouths of the caves were murderously hot. He and his men dared not even go in far enough to see how much material was there.

In the course of the next hour, Force 90 placed its explosives. Heavy charges were set to collapse the entrances to the caves; other large quantities had been tossed inside, to be detonated by timers, since no one would be foolhardy enough to venture inside the lethal environment.

At ten in the morning, when the sun beat down hard and hot on the valley, the explosives were detonated. The cave entrances collapsed, burying the radioactive materials inside. Then, as the timers counted down to zero, explosions went off inside the sealed caves, bursting the drums and rendering it impossible for anyone to excavate these sites in the next ten thousand years.

"Not exactly what the Iraqis had in mind, I guess." Bolan said after the last shock and puff of dust announced the burst of the last charge.

"I'm not so certain," Shondor replied. He nodded at Ali Ibrahim.

The Iraqi shepherd grinned and nodded. The valley and hills were once more safe for him and his goats.

11

The bar where Ilse von der Schulenberg danced was called Tiny's. As far as Napoleon Malik was concerned, it was as good a place as any to meet the members of the Islamic Strike Force who would provide muscle and gunpower for the coming operation. Also, it would give him a chance to check Ilse's discipline, to see if she would pretend not to recognize him, as were her orders.

Three young men appeared for his first meeting—Ahmed Hassan, a Palestinian enrolled as a student at the University of Southern California; Ismat Helmi, another student, studying at the University of Arizona; and an Iranian, Jani Zahedi, who had been granted political asylum in the United States and worked as a laboratory assistant for the Los Angeles County Department of Public Health.

They looked alike—small, wiry, intense, two of them dressed in light-colored double-breasted suits with white shirts and no neckties. They talked and thought alike. Malik saw that they were exactly what he had been when he was in his twenties—angry and full of hate, yet not quite sure what he was angry about or who he hated. They talked about imperialism and about freeing people from slavery to the capitalist system. Yet, plainly enough, their talk was only cant. In truth they cared nothing about freeing anybody from anything. He could understand, because he had talked this way himself, that the real problem for these young men was their frustrated envy. They saw others with power and wealth, and they wanted it.

They drank beer.

"This is prohibited, you know," Malik said to them as he lifted his own glass of Scotch and water. He referred to the Islamic law that forbade the faithful to drink alcohol.

Hassan laughed and raised his glass. "God doesn't know everything."

The others laughed. And that settled that. They were not religious, not of the faithful.

"Some time ago," Malik began, "each of you swore absolute allegiance to the Islamic Strike Force. But—" he shrugged "—men change. Young men especially. You were told when you swore allegiance that absolute loyalty and obedience would be required and that you would be disposed of, as would your families, if you didn't obey every order given you. Well, I'm about to give you some orders. Very hard orders. We're going to commit an act of historical significance. And I, right now, as the leader of the ISF, offer you a chance to get out. If your commitment has lessened, you may confess as much to me and leave. I release you from your obligation."

"Are we going to do what we did in Majorca? Only maybe ten thousand times over?" Helmi asked.

Malik nodded. "It may bring the imperialists to their knees. Or—"

"Or we may be totally and finally destroyed," Hassan finished. "I mean, my people, the Palestinians. And maybe others. In their rage the imperialists may—"

"Are you afraid?" Zahedi asked scornfully. "Or don't you have the stomach for unpleasant realities?"

Hassan sipped beer and calmly shook his head. "Our leader can tell you what stomach I have," he said. "Let him tell you about the bomb in Hebron."

Zahedi and Helmi looked curiously at Malik.

"Ahmed Hassan," Malik told them, "is the man who planted and fired the bomb in the Jewish hospital. You remember, I'm sure. He's the man. I wouldn't question his stomach for unpleasant work."

Zahedi stared for a moment at Hassan, showing a degree of admiration. "My apologies, Hassan. Each of us has done grisly work."

"There are only about eighty of us," Malik went on. "Did you know we are so few? And we suffered heavy casualties—very heavy casualties—within the past twenty-four hours in Iraq. We are an elite force. And—" he paused to reach across the table and place his hand on a hand of each of the young men in turn "—and those of us who survive will have not just the satisfaction of knowing we have changed the world, but some of the material benefits of terror and power. Hmm? You wouldn't turn away any of *those* benefits, would you?"

"Let's talk about what we're going to do," Hassan said somberly.

Malik nodded. "I think the three of you are enough. We'll work with a few others, my associates. But we—the four of us—*command*. Later we may have to eliminate the others, who may become inconvenient to us. Look at the young woman just mounting the stage to dance for us. She is German, a professional killer. She is one of us, for this operation."

Zahedi grinned. "I would like to be one with *her*."

"Easy enough to arrange, once you meet her," Malik replied. "But beware of our women. They're deadly. The late

Hajan Dihanesi scorned one of them—scorned her just a bit too much."

"A religious fool," said Zahedi, the Iranian. "We're well rid of him."

"I think we know what we're going to do," said Hassan. "Are we here to talk about the details?"

"We are," Malik agreed. "So, do you have the stomach, Hassan, to be effective a hundred times, maybe a thousand times, your effectiveness in Hebron?"

THAT EVENING Ahmed Hassan sat down in a bar on Sunset Boulevard with a young woman. He'd fallen in love with this young American named Jane Toller. She worked as a waitress in a hamburger joint and was on her break. She was a pallid blonde who seemed to make a point of never exposing her skin to the sun. She was also everything a small, muscular young man might dream of in a young woman—apart from being pale and blond, she was plump, busty and immodest. He'd never been in bed with her—maybe because he'd never asked her outright—but she had never denied the possibility.

"Jane," he said cautiously that evening, "is there some way...I mean, any way you can leave Los Angeles for a few days?"

"Hey, why would I want to do that? I mean, go where? And why?"

"Well, I..." He frowned and struggled within himself for a moment. "It is possible something bad is going to happen in Los Angeles. If so, I wouldn't want you to be here. You understand?"

"No, I don't understand at all. What's going to happen, Ahmed?"

"Something bad," he repeated.

She grinned. "The earthquake? Is that it, Ahmed? Do Palestinians have a special sense of when earthquakes are going to happen?"

He stared at her, almost tearful in his intensity. "Jane," he said hoarsely. "Just go. Take a vacation. Only…only out to San Bernardino, that will be far enough. But out of Los Angeles."

"For how long?" she asked.

"It is…it is Tuesday. For the rest of the week. That's all. For the rest of the week."

She laughed. "You're a crazy guy, but smart. So maybe I'll take your advice. Who knows? Maybe Palestinians do sense coming earthquakes."

FORCE 90 ARRIVED from Iraq a little after midnight. Though its existence, much less its achievement, could not be officially acknowledged, Hal Brognola met the plane at Otis Air Force Base and personally thanked each of the six men. He was introduced to them only as an unofficial spokesman for the President.

In a private room in the officers' mess a little while later Bolan, Savacheva and Brognola sat and talked.

"Good work, even the very best of work, wins us victories and never the war," Brognola said. "They're still going after a city. They've never changed objectives."

"New York?" Shondor asked.

"A vulnerable city, for sure," said Brognola. "But our indication is they're looking at Los Angeles."

"You got evidence for that?" Bolan queried.

"The FBI maintains surveillance on a number of people that fit the profile of potential terrorists. You know, young Middle Easterners probably entering the States as students, traveling alone. The FBI keeps an eye on young men and women who meet that profile."

"And in Los Angeles?" Bolan pressed.

"One of the possibles developed a crush on a waitress named Jane Toller. Lucky us, she's a parolee, recently released from the federal detention center in San Diego where she did two years of a five-year sentence for peddling substances. For some odd reason, she doesn't like being on parole and wants her final release."

"Imagine that," Shondor commented dryly.

"Okay. She has to tell her parole officer about anybody she dates, in advance, so she has to check out guys with the parole officer before she can accept an invitation. She gave the name Ahmed Hassan, the parole officer handed it to LAPD and they contacted the FBI."

"Bingo," Shondor said.

"Bingo is right. Ahmed Hassan is a Palestinian, in L.A. studying engineering at Southern Cal. Because of the profile, he's on a list. The FBI called on Jane Toller, and she's been reporting whatever this guy says to her. He talks a lot, tells her about his friends, where he goes, what he does. He tries to make himself look like a big man, but until Tuesday evening he never said anything to her that was worth hearing. Then Tuesday evening he told her to get out of Los Angeles. He said something bad was gonna happen there."

"Maybe he thinks there's going to be an earthquake," Shondor suggested.

Brognola shook his head. "He told her she'd be okay if she just went out as far as San Bernardino. If she can escape whatever he's got in mind just by going that far, he's not talking about an earthquake or an atomic explosion."

"But maybe about poisoning the water," Bolan said. "I bet San Bernardino isn't on the L.A. water system."

"Exactly. It isn't."

"It'd be harder to protect the L.A. water supply than th New York water supply," Bolan said. "L.A. gets water fror all over."

"Yes, but seventy-five percent of it comes in through th Los Angeles Aqueduct," Brognola replied. "The FBI ha already warned the L.A. authorities. They're patrolling da and night. Helicopters are over the aqueduct all the time But the aqueduct runs 338 miles."

"How much water does it carry?" Shondor asked.

"Depends. But usually around 450 million gallons a day."

"That would quickly dilute anything put in it," Shondo commented.

"Think of it as 18.75 million gallons per hour," Brog nola suggested. "Think of 312,000 gallons per minute. I say, the city's water supply is highly radioactive for twent minutes—"

"But surely it goes into a reservoir and then through treatment plant," Shondor said.

Brognola nodded. "Suppose they catch it and stop it be fore the radioactivity actually starts running through th water mains. The reservoirs where it's stopped, plus prot ably the treatment plants too, are dangerously contam nated—probably for years. A city can't live on twenty-fiv percent of its normal water supply. What's more, in larg parts of the city, the Los Angeles Aqueduct brings in *ninet percent* of the water supply." He paused and sighed. "If th United Righteous or anybody else introduces a large quar tity of cesium 137 into the Los Angeles Aqueduct, the cit will have to be evacuated."

"Abandoned," Shondor stated grimly.

"Abandoned," Brognola agreed. "there wouldn't eve be enough water to flush the sewage through the pipes."

"So Force 90 goes to California," Bolan said.

"With carte blanche," the big Fed replied. "Do whatever you have to do. LAPD is on the case, of course. The FBI, the Army. But you guys have your special ways. Do whatever you have to do."

ACCOMPANIED by an engineer from the Metropolitan Water District and Paul Lemaire, Bolan flew in a helicopter over the southern hundred miles of the aqueduct. Other teams from Force 90 covered other areas, not overlooking the fact that the threat could be to other aqueducts—the California Aqueduct coming down from Sacramento, or the Colorado River Aqueduct coming across from Arizona.

"It's got to be the Los Angeles Aqueduct, if L.A. is the target," Bolan said to Lemaire. "It's the only one that carries enough water to force evacuation of the city."

"The Los Angeles Aqueduct carries water that originates in snowmelt and rain in the Sierra Nevada," said the engineer, trying to be helpful. "It crosses deserts, passes through mountains, goes through 142 tunnels and crosses major canyons. It was an immense engineering project. Over most of its 338 miles, it runs on the surface. That's our big problem now—that so much of it runs on the surface."

Len Pasquale, the engineer, couldn't help but stare at the two men he was showing around the aqueduct. He'd been given an ambiguous idea of who they were—a team sent to save the city from disaster, and they could use whatever tough tactics were required. No questions asked. They were hard men sent to do a hard job.

The helicopter landed at the Burbank airport, and the three men—Bolan, Lemaire and Pasquale—were met by a Los Angeles police detective named Bob Verity.

Verity drove them north, roughly along the route of the aqueduct tunnel, though the roads didn't follow it, and on to the eastern slopes of the Tehachapi Mountains, where the aqueduct ran above ground.

The aqueduct was heavily guarded. Cars were turned away, and no one was allowed near.

As Bolan watched, two young men and a woman were ordered to turn back.

The two young men were Ahmed Hassan and Isma Helmi. The woman was Jasmin Malik.

"You can see it's not going to be easy," Hassan said. "I won't be a matter of simply coming to the edge of the water and dumping in our material."

"I see something a lot more ominous than that," Jasmin stated grimly. "They cannot—they do not—maintain this kind of security over the aqueduct at all times. They are on some kind of special alert. I wonder if our plan has been discovered."

"Betrayed?" Hassan asked.

"Discovered," she repeated. "I'd rather say discovered. Obviously we haven't been betrayed. If we were, they would have come after us. No. I think some element of our scheme has become known—just enough to raise suspicions and put them on alert."

ALBRECHT KIRCHNER arrived at the bar on La Cienega. For him, too, it was as good a place as any to meet. Ilse didn't pretend not to know him. After she had taken her turn on the stage, she went to his table and sat down. They spoke English with practiced American accents.

"You'll have to buy me a beer," she said, "and it'll cost you eight dollars."

He shrugged. "You're a charming dancer," he said sarcastically.

"You can go to hell. Are things shaping up?"

"Tonight, if all goes well, I take delivery of another eight kilograms of cesium 137."

"Malik was here," she informed him. "He's recruited three juveniles to carry the guns."

"Three experienced terrorists," Kirchner stressed. "Don't underestimate them."

"What about *our* people?"

"Two members of Red Nippon. Malik doesn't know about them. We'll leave it that way."

"Do they have the cesium?"

Kirchner frowned. He hadn't meant to tell her. But, since she had guessed... "It's what our late friend Isoroku Akada had accumulated. He wasn't going to put it in the Ohio River. He held it back from that operation. We've inherited it."

"So how much do we have to put in the aqueduct?"

"Let's say a hundred times what caused the disaster in Goiânia," Kirchner replied. "There they had to dig up streets and carry away and bury the contaminated pavement and soil."

"Enough, then." Her eyes glittered in anticipation. "It should be enough."

"We have another problem," Kirchner said. "The aqueduct is heavily guarded. The police and armed forces are blocking all access to it." He shrugged. "I'm confident we can find a way to do what we want to do. But this heavy security can only mean that our attack is expected. And that means something else—Bolan is in Los Angeles."

BOLAN PUT DOWN the pair of binoculars handed to him by LAPD Detective Bob Verity. He shook his head. "I don't recognize him."

"That's Hassan," Verity explained. "The girl behind the counter is Jane, the parolee he's got the hots for. She's the one he wants to get out of town before something bad happens."

"You're tailing him?" Bolan asked.

"I've got six men detailed to him," Verity replied. "Eight-hour shifts. Two men on each. Here's a report."

Bolan scanned a typewritten report of Ahmed Hassan' whereabouts for the day.

8:12 a.m. Left room, went to university, worked in lab.

9:43 a.m. Left lab, picked up by two unidentified subjects, one male, one female, both of dark complexion, female attractive.

9:43 a.m.-2:11 p.m. Three subjects in 1987 Ford, CA license FX 1423 T (Not stolen.) Drove north, general area of Edwards AFB, Mojave. No apparent purpose. Did not leave car except for comfort stop.

2:30 p.m. Seminar in electrical engineering, USC.

Bolan returned the report to Verity. "So they were north of the city where we were this morning. Looking at the aqueduct, you suppose?"

"I'd suppose," Verity agreed. "It seems too easy, though, doesn't it? Too damned easy. I mean, the only suspect we have—"

"Too easy. Hassan and his friends in the car can't be working alone. On the other hand they were out there looking at the aqueduct, the same thing we were doing."

"We won't touch him," Verity said.

"No. And whatever you do, don't lose him."

"Colonel Pollock, the guy who loses Hassan is going to drink the first glass of radioactive water that comes through the system."

ALBRECHT KIRCHNER MET the two members of Red Nippon at the Hyatt Regency on Wilshire Boulevard. Though they had the appearance of two visiting Japanese business-men—well-dressed, polite—Ugaki Ryu-ichi and Sakai Kenro were experienced killers, experts in martial arts and skilled in the use of a wide variety of deadly weapons.

Kirchner spoke no Japanese, and their English was weak. The conversation, consequently, was limited to a few basic things. The cesium was in their car. They had rented a garage in Azusa where the cesium could be removed from its capsules and loaded in whatever containers would be used to introduce it into the aqueduct. They themselves would be available to handle the radioactive material—or if the United Righteous had others who could do it, they would gladly stand aside. Also, they would serve as soldiers in the operation if they were needed.

The cesium wouldn't leave their custody until payment was made. They hoped this would be no problem, but their instructions from the late Isoroku Akada were to receive one million dollars in cash before turning over the radioactive material.

Kirchner agreed. Napoleon Malik had the money. At least he hoped he did. It was, of course, General Laqiya's money. Kirchner told the two Japanese that the money would be handed over before morning. Would they be so kind as to take the cesium to the garage in Azusa?

It was, perhaps, a measure of their self-confident ruth-lessness that they readily agreed to take the material to Azusa. Others might have feared betrayal, an ambush, a quick theft of the valuable cesium. Ryu-ichi and Kenro had no such fear.

ILSE HAD PLACED a call, summoning a man to the bar. Late in the afternoon he arrived.

"I never thought I would see you again," he said. "I'm not certain I am seeing you. I wouldn't have recognized you."

"Did Hesse pay you?" she asked.

The man, Tom Reynolds, sipped beer and looked past Ilse at the blond girl dancing on the stage. He wasn't out of place here, looking, as he did, like one of the American working-class men who like this bar—liked the dim lights, the smoky air, the topless dancing.

"I said, did Hesse pay you?"

Reynolds shook his head. "No, as a matter of fact. I was lucky to get out of that place alive. So were you."

"Where was he carrying the gun?" she asked. "How did it escape our search?"

"I don't know. He asked to go to the bathroom. I was going to give him an injection, as you know, and letting him relieve himself so he wouldn't do it when the shot relaxed him didn't seem like such a bad idea. So we let him go in the men's room. Joe went with him. The next thing I heard was a couple of pops, then two shots. He'd killed Joe. He killed Hesse. I ran and got away from him. Your Colonel Pollock was a tough man."

"He's back in town."

Reynolds frowned hard. "I wouldn't want to run into him."

"So shave off your beard. Anyway, I *want* you to run into him. We're going to finish the job."

Reynolds began to shake his head.

"I'll do it this time," she said. "I intend to take him out with a rifle. We won't have to get close to him, but I want you to find him for me. Working in this place is my cover, and to keep my cover good I've got to keep long hours here. Besides, this has become something of a meeting place for certain people. But you, you're not on everybody's most-wanted list. You can wander around all you want to.''

''In a town this size!''

''I want you to cover one place,'' she said. ''Just sit in a car and watch. That's all you have to do. Tonight. Maybe tomorrow night. I think I know where he might go.''

''Where?''

Ilse grinned. ''I'm going to bet there's a little bit of sentiment in the guy. He and I had a nice, romantic steak dinner in a restaurant on Sunset. I'm guessing he'll go back there. If he's not sentimental, anyway he loves a good steak. Maybe he's just bulldog enough to go someplace where he figures there's even the slightest chance he might run into me and jerk me into the slammer. All you gotta do is look for the guy. And call me if you see him.''

Reynolds nodded. ''Okay. Uh, like you asked me about, I never did get paid by Hesse. Y' know?''

''You'll get paid this time,'' she replied. ''It'll be a big payday if you find Colonel Pollock for me.''

''MY FRIEND, I am hungry,'' Paul Lemaire said. ''And thirsty. A man can't work effectively if he doesn't eat and drink. Or hadn't you noticed this?''

Bolan looked up from a map of the county, a detailed chart with the aqueducts, reservoirs, well fields, treatment plants and principal water mains marked. He shook his head.

''It's true,'' Verity added. ''For an hour I've been listening to your bellies rumbling. Anyway, you know, there's nothing you can do here. Let the guys who know the town study the possibilities. It's only when those bastards move, or if we get a clue of some kind that you can help us. When that time comes, I'd rather have guys on my side who aren't half starved. Just let me know where you're going to be, and if anything breaks you'll know about it ASAP.''

Bolan stood up and flexed his muscles. "I guess you've got a point."

"Where'll you be?"

Bolan looked at Lemaire. "What kind of food do you want, Paul?"

"American, of course," the Frenchman replied. "The steaks rare, the chicken fried, the tomato sauce poured on the *pommes frites*. All that."

"Okay. There's a place on Sunset called Marietta's. I had a great steak there one time, and there's a remote possibility that somebody I'd like to see might show up there."

UGAKI RYU-ICHI NODDED with pronounced solemnity. "It is well to be brave," he said quietly. "It is well to hate. It is better to plan intelligently and to execute an intelligently conceived plan."

Ryu-ichi's face was thin, his cheeks hollow. His black hair was silvered at the temples, and he wore steel-rimmed eyeglasses. So grave was his face that Kirchner wondered if he ever smiled, wondered if it were even possible for those thin lips to form a smile.

He continued. "So far you have succeeded in killing some people in two luxury hotels, plus impeding the Rhine traffic for a few days. I will not sell you the cesium for any price unless you demonstrate to me that you know how to use it effectively."

Napoleon Malik was angry, but he knew it would be a serious mistake to show his anger. "We're going to put it in the Los Angeles Aqueduct."

"How?" Ryu-ichi asked.

"We aren't certain yet. They're obsessively alert. The route of the aqueduct is guarded by police and troops."

Ryu-ichi nodded. "Precisely. As it was not, only a few days ago. Something clumsy has been done."

Sakai Kenro nodded his agreement.

"How much money do you have?" Ryu-ichi asked. "The Sidian lunatic has provided a great deal, I understand."

Kirchner glanced at Malik.

"We have the million you asked for," Malik replied.

"The price is now one and one-half million," Ryu-ichi said coldly. "One million for the material itself. Half a million for showing you how to put it in the aqueduct."

"We know how to put it in the aqueduct," Malik replied.

"Yes? How? How will you get past the guards? How will you prevent their knowing the material is in the water and shutting the gates?"

"We have—"

"You have yet to discover the means," Ryu-ichi mocked. "We know *where* to put it in and *how*."

"That is easy to say," Kirchner scoffed.

Ryu-ichi bowed. "A demonstration."

They were meeting in the garage in Azusa, where the two Japanese—and most likely backup who remained out of sight—had established a small engineering shop and a laboratory. In the center of the floor stood a large water tank, open at the top like a tank used to water cattle. It contained about three or four gallons of water. Kenro walked to a work bench and picked up a metal cylinder eighteen inches long and ten inches in diameter. It was obviously heavy, as they could see him struggling with the weight as he carried it to the tank.

Ryu-ichi nodded, and Kenro dropped the cylinder in the tank.

After a moment it exploded, throwing water out of the tank and wetting Malik and Kirchner. But lying on the bottom, after the explosion, was a green capsule, substantially smaller than the cylinder. Two halves of the lead-lined cylinder lay to the sides.

Ryu-ichi looked at his watch. "Ah, now. We need some minutes."

He walked to a table at one end of the room and poured himself a drink. By gesture he offered drinks to the others.

"The final question is, *where*," Ryu-ichi announced. "Where can one gain access to the aqueduct? If you gentlemen had come here six weeks ago, instead of a few days before you expect to poison the water, you would have had time to explore the entire route of the aqueduct. As we have done."

"So...where?" Kirchner asked.

Ryu-ichi nodded gravely. "When our transaction has been completed, we will show you. Perhaps we should now look in the bottom of our tank."

They walked to the tank and peered in. The green plastic capsule had dissolved, leaving only small pieces. Shortly it would dissolve completely, disappear.

"Water first dissolved the plug that held the electric switch open," Ryu-ichi explained. "That allowed the switch to close and a small current to pass from the battery pack and detonate a small quantity of plastic explosive—just enough to split the lead-lined cylinder. The green capsule was then exposed to water, and in a few minutes *it* dissolved. If it had been filled with cesium 137, the cesium would be free in the water."

"The capsule," Kenro added, "will move with the fast flow of water in the aqueduct. By the time it dissolves, the cesium will be in the Los Angeles water system, beyond where a gate could be closed against it."

"How many capsules will it take to disperse the amount of cesium we have?" Malik asked.

"Twenty—combining your cesium and ours."

"But guards will see the capsules in the water," Kirchner objected. "They'll hear the explosions."

Ryu-ichi shook his head. "Not where we will introduce the cylinders into the aqueduct—*inside a tunnel!*"

For the first time the faint suggestion of a smile crept across the face of Ugaki Ryu-ichi.

GENERATIONS of tourists had explored Sunset Boulevard. Now, most of the attraction was gone from this stretch. The famous Body Shop was still open, offering still another year of strip shows, but the excitement that had once made the Strip special was mostly gone.

Marietta's Steak House served food on the site of what had once been a lively nightclub.

Ilse sat in a steel-gray Honda Civic in a parking lot across the street and assembled her rifle. She was dressed in tight black pants and a black cotton sweater. In her small plastic purse she carried the snub-nose Smith & Wesson .357 Magnum she'd bought in Arizona.

Jasmin Malik was on the street outside Marietta's. Ilse had been humiliated by her failure to get Bolan the first time he tried, and this time she'd decided to let the exotic Pakistani bear some of the responsibility. It was, in the fist place, Jasmin's assignment. In the second place, if they succeeded here would be enough glory for both of them.

They had talked. Ilse would take a shot from across the street. If she missed, or if something else went wrong, Jasmin would make an attempt with her silenced 9 mm Taurus. If necessary, Ilse could take another shot with the rifle, or cross the street and fire at close range with the .357.

There were, after all, only two men to deal with, as Reynolds had reported. Colonel Pollock, which was all the

name Reynolds had for him, had gone into Marietta's wit
one other man, a short, paunchy man smoking a cigarette

Jasmin walked up and down the street, conspicuousl
impatient. She wore a short black skirt and a white blouse
with shiny black high-heeled shoes. She looked like a Mex
ican in Ilse's judgment. Apparently she looked like some
thing else, too, since two men had stopped their cars at th
curb and tried to pick her up.

Ilse didn't know two important facts—first, that Bola
was accompanied not just by one man but by two; second
that Marietta's was under surveillance by LAPD. Lieuten
ant Bob Verity had gone to the steak house about half a
hour after Bolan and Lemaire arrived. He, too, was hun
gry. He and headquarters might have to communicate at an
time, and on a secure line, so an LAPD communication
van was standing by, with scrambled radio on a special fre
quency. Because the lieutenant and the communications va
were there, a black-and-white with two uniformed officer
cruised the street.

As NINE APPROACHED, Jane Toller kept glancing back an
forth between the clock on the wall behind the counter an
her watch. They never seemed to agree. She could hav
sworn the manager set the wall clocks back during a shift t
get five more minutes out of the staff. She scooped up he
purse as she caught sight of Hassan waiting outside.

"You should have a drink with me," he suggested whe
she joined him.

"I'm pooped, buddy."

"I got to tell you something."

She sighed. "Like what, Ahmed?"

Suddenly she realized it might be about getting out of Lo
Angeles before "something bad" happened. If he was righ
and something was going to happen, maybe she should g

out like he said. Or maybe he was going to tell her something the FBI would like to know.

"A nice drink," he said. "Like in the bar at Marietta's."

She looked down at herself. She'd changed from her uniform into a pair of blue shorts and a polo shirt.

"Hey, Ahmed," she said. "I don't think they'd let me in the bar at Marietta's."

He smiled. "They'll let you. I promise."

Ten minutes later they sat in a booth in the bar of the steak house. She'd seen Hassan hand the chief a ten-dollar bill and wondered what was so important.

About the same time, Bolan received his change from the cash he'd handed the waitress to pay for three steak dinners—and wine for Lemaire.

The Frenchman was happy, as he often was after a good dinner accompanied by red wine. On the way out they stopped at the cashier's counter, where Lemaire wanted to pick up a book of matches.

"Hold it," Verity whispered to Bolan. "Glance at the third booth in the bar. That's our friend Ahmed Hassan."

Bolan looked over casually. "Would the girl be Jane Toller?"

Verity nodded.

"Interesting," Bolan said. "Can we suppose, then, that nothing's going to happen tonight? She's still in town."

THE POLICE CRUISER had passed by Marietta's six times in the past half hour, and the officers inside had taken note of Jasmin Malik, still conspicuously on the street.

"Hey, girl. Hold it right there."

Jasmin turned and glared at the two men in the police car.

"I have a question or two," said Officer Drake McDougal, "and I'd like to see some ID."

"You ask *this*?" she protested shrilly. "What is for, this?"

Jasmin Malik was terrified, and in her fear her English—weak at best—failed her.

"All I want is an ID. Driver's license, green card, whatever. You got a passport?"

She turned and walked away from the policeman, which was a mistake. He grabbed her by the arm, and Jasmin turned on him with all the fury of a woman wronged, wrath in her eyes, and swung toward him with her fists.

"Hey, *honey*, for God's sake!"

Officer McDougal had more experience than he wanted with women who went into hysterics. He had turned her around and was locking her hands behind her back before his partner ran over and helped.

"Hey, what we got here?" McDougal asked as he checked inside her purse. "A . . . what the hell kind of peashooter is this? Son of a bitch! *Silenced*, yet."

McDougal's partner got on the radio. "Uh, Car 8456. We're assigned to Bob Verity, Sunset, front of Marietta's. Got a suspected hooker who turns out to be carrying heat. Silenced. Foreign make. Advise."

"Car 8456, hold suspect for vice. We'll advise Lieutenant Verity you have extra problem."

"Roger. Suspect apparently foreign national. Uh, indeterminate. Carrying no documents. Repeat, no documents. Do not take suspect for Hispanic. More likely Middle East."

"Correct on hold for vice, 8456. Hold for special unit. Hold damned sure. Be alert for hidden weapons. Regard suspect as dangerous in extreme."

"Roger."

Ilse had watched the arrest of Jasmin from across the street. Suddenly she was aware of something—that this block of Sunset Boulevard was alive with police. She had no chance of taking out Bolan unless she was willing to die in the attempt.

Ilse von der Schulenberg had no intention of throwing her life away.

12

Ahmed Hassan had left Jane Toller on the street in front of Marietta's and hurried away. Within a minute the woman was arrested for interrogation.

"I swear he said nothing. Hey! Could I have called you? Come on! He shows up at McDonald's, picks me up in the parking lot, brings me here. Come on, guys! Take the damned cuffs off. What the hell. I've been cooperating with you. Besides, they're too tight. All he said was for me to get out of town. Something bad's going to happen. And you guys rousted me before I could get to a phone and tell you."

They took her in and put her in a cell two doors down the line from Jasmin.

She became frightened. "Hey! If something bad's going to happen in Los Angeles, you can't keep me here! Come on! Hey, come on!"

AHMED HASSAN WALKED east on Sunset Boulevard, unaware of the arrest of Jasmin Malik and Jane Toller. He was unaware also that he was the subject of a heavy surveillance by a growing number of police officers of LAPD, plus Bolan and Lemaire, who followed him on foot, one on each side of the street and half a block behind.

Ilse followed, too. She'd noticed the police following Hassan, so she cautiously kept her distance, driving the gray

Honda ahead, stopping, letting Hassan pass, and waiting as long as she dared before moving on again.

Kirchner didn't know where she was nor did she know where he was. Or Malik. She couldn't phone them to tell them Jasmin had been arrested, couldn't warn them that Hassan was being followed. It was impossible to tip off Hassan, and she couldn't take a shot at Bolan, though he was on the street, an easy target.

Bolan kept to the opposite side of the street from Hassan, while Lemaire followed on the same side. The Arab walked briskly, purposefully. He kept to Sunset for three blocks, then crossed the street and turned south. A half block later he reached a parking lot, jogged over to the dark blue Ford van, unlocked it and climbed in.

Verity's driver pulled up beside Bolan, then beside Lemaire, and they got into the unmarked police car.

Central dispatch was already reporting a computer check on the license plates on the van, which belonged to a rental agency.

"Something's coming down," Verity said. "Hassan never had a car before. Now he's got a van."

The young man paid for his parking, then drove back to Sunset Boulevard, where he turned east. Curt, crisp radio commands directed the police pursuit. Eight blocks east on Sunset, when Hassan stopped for a traffic light, a pedestrian casually walked behind the van. The pedestrian—a plainclothes woman—slapped the rear bumper, leaving a tiny radio transmitter magnetically attached. Two helicopters reported that they had the vehicle in sight, but they stayed well up and away. The transmitter made tracking easier. The helicopters and several of the cars could home on it.

Hassan entered the Hollywood Freeway, staying with only to the intersection of the Pasadena Freeway, where h turned northeast. Shortly he passed Dodger Stadium.

Four unmarked police cars kept within a hundred yard of the dark blue Ford. If anyone noticed that a steel-gra Honda Civic had joined the pursuit and kept up, no one a tached any significance to it.

IN THE GARAGE in Azusa, Ugaki Ryu-ichi and Sakai Kenr finished counting the money and stuffed the last o $1,500,000 into a third suitcase. Ryu-ichi was satisfied, an Sakai Kenro began loading the rest of the cesium into th water-soluble capsules and lead cylinders.

Ismat Helmi and Jani Zahedi were there with Kirchne and Malik. For half an hour they watched the two Japanes methodically pushing money into suitcases. To one sid Zahedi quietly asked Malik if the ISF was really going to le all the money go, or would they pull guns on the tw Japanese and take it back as soon as they had the details o the plan for introducing the cesium into the Los Angele water system. Malik shook his head and answered tha nobody double-crossed Red Nippon and lived, not eve soldiers of ISF.

Malik had brought the capsules of cesium 137 that Ils von der Schulenberg had smuggled into the Unites States The capsules were made of lead and platinum, and now the had to be opened so that the deadly radioactive cesium coul be transferred to the small bombs the Japanese had de vised.

The Japanese had built a facility for performing that task It was a lead-shielded compartment about four feet squar and six feet high. Inside were the tools for opening the lead and-platinum containers and pouring the cesium into its ne containers. These tools were activated and manipulate rom outside by electrical switches and rods that ran through he walls of the compartment. Two small color television ameras were mounted inside the compartment, with monitors outside, so the work could be watched.

Sakai Kenro had devised the machinery, and he manipuated it. He put the first lead-and-platinum container in a lamp and tightened it. Then he activated a small electrical machine that moved a hacksaw blade back and forth. Using a control rod, he brought the blade down on the top of he container. Slowly the blade bit into the capsule. When t had cut a deep notch but not yet penetrated as far as the esium, Kenro stopped.

During the work on the first container, everyone stared at he monitors. They saw that the clamp was hinged and that Kenro could turn the two ends, breaking the container in wo on the sawed notch.

Beneath the clamps was a teflon-lined funnel. The spout of the funnel ran into one of the water-soluble capsules. When the capsule broke, the cesium powder fell into the unnel and ran down into the waiting capsule.

Kenro used rods to shake the whole apparatus, then to tap t, to make sure every trace of the cesium ran down into the apsule. When he was satisfied, he used other rods to press cap onto the capsule, to move it and drop it into a lead ylinder. He pressed a lead cap onto the cylinder. Finally he noved the empty capsule to a lead box, opened it, dropped a the empty but radioactive capsule and closed the lid.

Even with the caution he exercised, Kenro carried a geiger counter into the compartment when he entered. He vore a lead apron and lead gloves. The counter clicked a ttle, but the compartment remained essentially clean. Kenro tightened the cap on each cylinder and carried it outide.

He required less than ten minutes on each transfer of material.

"Now that he sees how your containers are constructed it will go faster," Ryu-ichi said after Malik and Kirchner watched Kenro load the first bomb. "Would you like to know where the cylinders are to be dropped into the aqueduct?"

Kirchner and Malik were very anxious to know, and Ryu-ichi led them to a desk on the side of the room farthest from the lead-lined compartment. There he showed them a detailed map of the northern reaches of the water system.

"In tunnel, yes?" he said. "The aqueduct runs in a deep tunnel through the mountains, under the forest. But a tunnel must have access to the surface at intervals. It must be possible for air to move in and out. So, there are air shafts. You will find they are not guarded as the surface aqueduct is. I went out and looked this afternoon. No police. No soldiers. You will have to use a small quantity of explosives to blow the screened top off one of the air shafts, but when you have done that you can drop your cylinders down the shaft. They will fall into the water, their little charges will detonate and your cesium will be rushing toward the city in rapidly dissolving capsules."

Kirchner nodded enthusiastic approval. "Brilliant."

Ryu-ichi accepted the compliment without the least change of expression. He bowed slightly.

Malik looked at his watch. Jasmin had known where to come and hadn't shown up. He had sent Helmi to Tiny's to pick up Ilse, and the young Jordanian had reported that she wasn't there. Not only that, but she had been fired by the owner for walking away from her job without permission. It was difficult to imagine where the two women were.

Hassan, too, was late, and he was supposed to be bringing the van that would carry the twenty cesium bombs.

Kenro was all but finished. Helmi and Zahedi were attaching the small explosive charges that would split the lead casings, in the way Kenro had showed them.

Malik had something to worry about. Where were his people?

Maybe he ought to move as fast as possible. Something was wrong. He had one advantage—none of the missing people knew where the cesium was going. And he could carry it in two or three cars.

COMING OFF THE NORTH end of the Pasadena Freeway, Hassan entered the eastbound lane of the Colorado Freeway. Ten minutes later he reached the garage where Malik and Kirchner were waiting.

The other members of Force 90 were on their way, alerted by police radio. The helicopters kept their distance, their powerful searchlights dark. Following only the taillights of the van and homing on its radio signal, they pinpointed the vehicle for the pursuing police cars. The cars dropped off a block or two short of the garage and began cruising the area while awaiting further orders.

Ilse didn't have the advantage of tuning in the homing transmitter, nor could she listen in on the conversations between the helicopters and the ground. She lost the van three or four blocks from the garage and began to cruise, looking for it.

In the unmarked police car, stopped a block away, Bolan talked with Captain Kenneth Drake who was at police headquarters.

"Looks like we won't need your backup, Colonel," the captain said. "We can handle it from here."

"Can't agree with you on that, Captain. My guys are specialists, picked for this very job. Besides, we operate covertly. You move in here, sooner or later you're going to

have to explain what you were doing—to the televisio
cameras, to the newspapers. We won't. We'll be gone, a
we'll take our mess with us. And if we make a mistake, i
on our heads, not yours.''

''You make a powerful argument,'' Drake replied.

''If you can block off the area, keep people away, we
take on the terrorists. And don't forget, Captain, these gu
are terrorists and they don't come any tougher.''

''Okay, Colonel. You've made your case. We'll sta
back and let you take it.''

''That's what we're here for.''

The police moved fast to evacuate the houses in t
neighborhood of the garage. Even so, by the time Force
could move into place, fourteen of the cesium bombs we
in the Ford van, three were in each of two cars and the m
of the United Righteous were gathering their weapons a
getting ready to move out.

Bolan led Oberfallen and Syrkin along the street towa
the front of the garage. Shondor, Lemaire and Balduc
strode up an alley to the rear to cover a back door.

''Colonel Pollock—''

A message came over the Handie-Talkie clipped to B
lan's web belt.

''Colonel, an across-the-street neighbor that we ev
cuated reports they carried a lot of heavy cylinders out a
loaded them into the van.''

''Roger, and thanks.''

He spoke to Syrkin. ''What better way to announce ou
selves than by making sure that van isn't going anywhere?

He raised his G-11 to his shoulder and took aim on t
hood of the Ford. Four quick squeezes of the trigger sent
round bursts smashing into the van. Caseless bullets d
signed to pierce a steel helmet easily punctured the sheet ste
of the van and tore into the engine compartment, instant

blasting the carburetor to pieces, together with the distributor and coil. The van wouldn't be moving.

Syrkin followed with a 3-round burst into the rear left wheel, shredding the tire.

For a long moment there was no reaction from the garage. It was as if the assault had been sent to the wrong address, and there was no one in the concrete-block building other than astonished and frightened mechanics. Then a burst of automatic gunfire tore away a steel window frame and blew away its glass. Someone tossed a small, square package through the opening, and it flew over the disabled van and the cars parked in front of the garage, and landed in the street.

"Bomb!" Bolan yelled.

Everyone dropped to the ground, and a second later the bomb exploded with an immense roar. The concussion swept over the prone men, carrying with it a storm of small gravel and street debris, which didn't injure anyone.

In seconds Bolan was up, charging across the street and into cover behind the Ford van. He paused briefly to fire a burst through the shattered window of the garage, then, having driven whoever was behind that window to the floor, he threw an MU-50 grenade.

The deadly orb sailed through the opening and fell inside the garage. The explosion shot steel pellets through the building, some of them blowing glass from another window.

Syrkin and Oberfallen had rushed the building, too. The German crouched beside Bolan behind the van; the Israeli was shielded from the building by a red Toyota parked to the right of the van.

They could hear the sound of gunfire behind the garage. Force 90's second team was in action.

Streams of slugs chopped the blacktop of the driveway. Two or three gunners were pouring lead from the shattered front windows. Obviously the grenades hadn't silenced the guns inside the garage.

Bolan rose to throw a second grenade, but Oberfallen had already stood and tossed one through the window. Then he fell to the ground, hit. Hit from behind? The Executioner dropped to a crouch and peered into the darkness across the street. Between those houses?

The German rolled back against the van and groaned in pain. He had been hit in the leg, and the bullet had ripped away a lot of flesh and muscle. Even so, he gave Bolan a thumbs-up sign and managed a weak grin. He began binding his leg with his web belt—a tourniquet to staunch the gushing blood.

When Oberfallen's grenade exploded in the garage, Syrkin tossed in another and ran to the window. As soon as his grenade exploded, he thrust the muzzle of his G-11 through the window and sprayed the interior with small, high-velocity slugs.

Bolan could hear the Israeli's burst ricocheting inside the little building, whining and cracking. When Syrkin dropped back to reload, the warrior rushed forward and fired into the garage.

The slug hit the wall just to his right. Somebody *was* shooting from across the street. He moved to put the body of the van between him and the unseen assailant.

"Between the houses," Oberfallen muttered.

INSIDE THE GARAGE, Zahedi was dead. So was Kenro. Kirchner was bleeding from wounds to the head. Grenade pellets had hit him, luckily above the eye. An inch lower and they would have blinded him.

Ryu-ichi crouched beside Malik. They had taken temporary refuge inside the lead-lined compartment. It afforded protection against almost anything.

"We have an advantage," Ryu-ichi said to Malik.

Battle wasn't Malik's forte. He was terrified and hadn't fired a shot. "What is it?" he asked.

"The cesium. If the containers in the van can be broken open and the cesium scattered by an explosion..."

Malik nodded.

"Gather up all the plastique," Ryu-ichi directed. "All of it. I never thought much about what cesium 137 would do if blown into the air. It won't do what it would have done in the water, but on tonight's wind it will drift into Glendora. Maybe as far as San Bernardino. We are going to die, my friend. But maybe not for nothing."

Ryu-ichi crawled out of the compartment, over the body of Kenro, and picked up an Uzi.

"Malik,' he said coldly. "Come out here and fight. Or I will cut you down *now*."

BOLAN KNELT beside Oberfallen. He had seen wounds like this before; the slug had exploded. Whoever was across the street was firing explosive-tipped rounds.

The radio crackled. "Colonel Pollock, this is Shondor. Balducci is down. Lemaire's hit but can still fire. I'm okay myself."

"Roger. Listen for my attack in front, then support it."

"Roger."

Bolan put down the G-11. He leveled the Desert Eagle on the double doors of the garage and fired five heavy slugs.

"Colonel!" Oberfallen yelled.

Bolan swung around just in time to see the figure between the two houses, and he had just enough time to drop before he saw the flash from a muzzle. A bullet exploded against the sheet metal of the van.

He raised the .44 Magnum and fired two shots into the darkness between the houses. He couldn't tell if he'd hit anything. The figure had vanished in the dark—hit or maybe not hit. There was no way to tell.

"On the roof!"

Bolan jerked around and looked up. Oberfallen was warning him about a man on the roof of the garage. The man stood silhouetted against the city glow of the sky, a black figure, arms above his head, ready to throw something.

The Executioner grabbed the G-11 and shot from the hip—he didn't have time to raise the rifle to his shoulder.

The apparition on the roof was lifted off his feet by a spray of high-velocity, high-power slugs. He fell backward, and whatever he had held above his head fell back with him.

The roof of the garage rose on a column of fire, lifted by an enormously powerful explosion. At the same time, the roof was driven down, to collapse into the building.

Without waiting for orders, Syrkin rushed into the garage, spraying the dark interior of the garage with a steady stream from his G-ll. Behind the building Shondor cut down Napoleon Malik, who was trying to escape out the back door.

Bolan brushed past Syrkin and strode into the center of the garage. He didn't know the identity of most of the men who had gathered in the garage, but none of them had survived.

THE EXECUTIONER walked out into the fresh night air, glad to escape the stench of burned explosive, gunfire and death. He went over to the van and looked inside at the deadly cylinders filled with cesium 137.

A bullet suddenly exploded against the flesh just under the warrior's left arm. Most of the fragmented slug glanced away and hit the side of the van, but it left a fiery, bleeding furrow.

Bolan dived to the ground, drawing the Desert Eagle.

Ilse had tossed her rifle aside and now leveled the muzzle of a revolver.

Suddenly she rose off the ground, like a marionette jerked up on its strings, as a hundred bullets chopped through her. Shondor and Syrkin didn't stop firing their weapons until Ilse von der Schulenberg was a lifeless shattered corpse.

DON PENDLETON's
MACK BOLAN ®

Backlash

Mack Bolan kicks open a hornet's nest when he discovers a
Nicaraguan power monger has been running drugs off the coast
of Miami to finance an overthrow of the Sandinista regime...and
has had a lot of help from the CIA.

Now the Company wants out and calls on the one man who can
salvage this operation gone haywire...THE EXECUTIONER!

Take
4 explosive books
plus a
mystery bonus
FREE